The girl saw Clint and began to run. . . .

"What's the matter, Jenny?" Clint shouted after her. "Are you still worried about being seen with me? Look, I'm sorry!"

Running after her, Clint grabbed her by the arm. "Help!" she screamed. "Call the sheriff!"

Clint suddenly heard a man yell, "Jenny, drop to the ground!" The girl fell as if she had been poleaxed, and as Clint twisted around, the sheriff and his deputies opened fire.

"Wait, there's been a mis—"

Clint felt hot lead whip past his face and knew this was no time for explanations. . . .

Don't miss any of the lusty, hard-riding action
in the Charter Western series, THE GUNSMITH

And coming next month:
THE GUNSMITH #56: WALKING DEAD MAN

THE GUNSMITH

55

THE LEGEND MAKER

J.R. ROBERTS

CHARTER BOOKS, NEW YORK

THE GUNSMITH #55: THE LEGEND MAKER

A Charter Book/published by arrangement with
the author

PRINTING HISTORY
Charter edition/July 1986

ISBN: 0-441-30959-3

Charter Books are published by The Berkley Publishing Group,
200 Madison Avenue, New York, New York 10016.
PRINTED IN THE UNITED STATES OF AMERICA

ONE

It was June and the air was hot and still. There was a feeling of death on the run as the Gunsmith guided his horse quickly through the brush and around great clumps of cactus. Clint Adams was not sure how many riders were following him, but he knew he was in trouble. Out in this hard, desert country just north of the Mexican border, a man had better know the lay of the land and be prepared to fight to kill because there was no quarter given by the Apache or the Mexican bandits—and none expected.

Night was falling across the land, but the air did not cool. Clint had been down in Mexico visiting some friends, and there had been a beautiful woman in Nogales who had fired his blood and held him too long. Now, the temperature was over one hundred. It was a good thirty miles to the nearest settlement and that was just too damned far to run Duke in this heat without a lot of water.

The choice was painfully simple. He could run his black gelding to death, putting himself out of danger, and then finish the last part of his trip to Tucson by stage, or he could fight and hope that the odds were not overwhelming. Hell, he thought, that is no decision at all—I will fight.

Clint waited until it was dark and then he began to search the shadows for a place to make his stand. He rode another two miles, feeling the riders behind him closing. Yet his pace did not quicken for if he began to run, they would know he was aware of their presence and that would rob him of the element of surprise.

Clint found a dry creek bed and rode up it, keeping to the rocky center where it would be difficult for even the best of trackers to follow his trail by moonlight. He waited until he found another creek bed that converged with the one he had been following, and he entered still keeping to the rocks. Overhead, the sky was cloudless, the stars a field of diamonds scattered across a jeweler's black velvet cloth. A long, sickle-shaped moon hung with a sharp cutting edge that glittered like polished gold.

He found a steep path out of the deep wash and Duke scrambled up its crumbled side. When they were on top and looking down, Clint dismounted. He was a gunfighter, and now he unwrapped the second pistol from his bedroll and shoved it into his waistband. He knew the gun was ready; it was a perfect match for the one that he wore on his hip. That gave him twelve shots. In country like this, a man did not have the luxury of letting his hammer rest on an empty cylinder.

Clint could hear them coming, their horses' hooves clopped loudly over the rocks that he had forced them to cover, and the sound of steel on rock told him that these were not the unshod ponies of the Apache, but rather the shod horses of the Mexican bandits who plagued this lawless southwestern frontier country. He heard a sound, and though it was really a hissed command still too distant to be understood, Clint could tell that it was Spanish. That confirmed his assessment of who was out to rob and kill him for his horse and whatever money and weapons he carried.

This bit of knowledge made him rest easier, not because the Mexicans were any less deadly, but becaus they did not fight with the crazed passion of the Apache and, if wounded, were much more inclined to retreat than to attack in a blood lust.

But how many? That was the critical question. He tried to tell by the sound of their horses' hooves, but that was impossible. He decided that he had better get his rifle from his saddle scabbard.

Duke nickered softly. He rubbed the animal's neck and whispered in its ear, "Stick around, old friend. If they are a small army, we may have to run a while longer until I can figure out a better plan than this one."

Clint moved back to the edge of the wash, and now he lay fully outstretched on his belly with a gun resting loosely in each fist and his Winchester rifle close beside him. When the sounds of the horses grew very near, he thought about how this was as good a place as he could have found on short notice. The Mexicans would be trapped in the wash and unable to charge up the side to reach him. They would have to go forward or back and then try to get him from the side; he would make them pay no matter the direction they chose.

It was almost impossible to see down into the wash, but when the bandits came around a bend, Clint took a quick estimate and guessed there were at least twenty. He swallowed, took a deep breath, and waited until they were almost directly below. Then, without warning, he opened fire with the speed and accuracy that had earned him a reputation as one of the deadliest men. Before the Mexicans realized it, four horses were bucking empty saddles, and by the time they could react, six of them were dead or wounded. Clint was swapping guns so fast that there was barely a break in the rolling thunder of his volley. The fresh Colt in his fist belched fire as the Mexicans shouted and died. They tried to attack, only to be thrown back by the steep walls.

The bandits split, some racing up the wash and some retreating. Clint rolled back from the wash, ejected his spent shells, and took the time to reload one of his guns. He grabbed his rifle, swung onto Duke, and raced away a hundred yards. Then he dismounted on the run just as the bandits came sweeping in from both sides.

Clint opened fire and knocked three more into the brush before they saw him standing a short distance from his horse. The last bunch of them charged, and he dropped to one knee, feeling their probing bullets seeking him out and seeing the red eyes of their fear-crazed horses reflecting moonlight. He thought that there might be seven or eight of them left. He did not have that many bullets remaining in his pistol, and he thought that this might be the end.

A bullet tore its bloody path across the muscles of his upper arm and spun him sideways, but the gun in his hand never wavered until it was empty. He had missed some shots because of the poor light, and now he grabbed the Winchester knowing there was no time to think, only to fight. The rifle bellowed with smoke and fire, and the lead bandit was hurled over backward from his saddle. That broke the ranks and the courage of his followers and sent the last of them whipping their horses off through the spiney cactus and thorny brush.

He heard their terrible curses in the night as they raced away. Clint listened to the drum of their horses' hooves receding in the night. Close by, he heard a low moan and wearily trudged to the man he had blown out of the saddle during that last charge. When the bandit realized Clint was standing over him, he covered his face, made the sign of the cross, and cried out in Spanish.

Clint knew enough Spanish to know that it meant God, save my life!

He took a deep breath and let it out slowly. "It is too late for you now," Clint said.

The bandit shivered, his hand slipped away from his face, and Clint saw him die.

He reloaded his pistols, knowing that tomorrow he might again be attacked, but not by the retreating survivors of this band. Clint stepped into the saddle and reined Duke north again.

Looking up, it seemed to him that the moon had changed from gold to red—a blood moon. He shook his head sadly and rode on toward Tucson.

TWO

The Gunsmith could see the outskirts of Tucson shimmering through the distant heat waves just ahead. Clint Adams pulled off his Stetson, sleeved his forehead dry, and then slapped the Stetson against his leg, creating a cloud of dust. He replaced his hat and then said to his horse, "We'll hole up in Tucson a couple of days just to rest and then we are pushing out of this desert, old friend. I know a mountain paradise where the grass is high, trout are always hungry in a cool, blue lake, and it never gets over eighty degrees all summer long. How does that sound?"

In answer, Duke tossed his head and continued across the desert. The trail north from Nogales had been uneventful after that one attack, but now both man and horse were eager to rest. Clint could see that Tucson was flourishing as he entered the main street. He sought out a livery where he could board his horse. The dusty streets were filled with freight wagons, and new buildings were going up everywhere.

Clint passed several inviting saloons and swallowed dryly at the thought of a cool beer; he envied the men he saw reclining in shade with painted ladies resting on their laps. Despite his beard and rough appearance, all of those women smiled and followed him with their eyes. Clint was amused but not enticed by those who called out to him: "Come on back, cowboy, and show me your pistol!"

They were prostitutes trolling for business and he

6

simply was not of a mind to pay for what he figured ought to be mutual pleasure between a man and woman. Besides, in this heat and at this hour, a beer and a nice shady place sounded even better than a hot woman.

He passed several livery stables but did not turn in after quick inspections. In one, the horses were too thin, indicating that the livery owner was stingy and cutting corners on his feed bills; in another, the stalls were unclean and the flies thick. Clint was mighty fussy about who kept Duke. The animal had saved his life many times and it deserved the best care available. But he finally located a first-class stable where the horses were fed well and sleek from brushing. The stalls were filled with fresh, clean straw. The board was four bits a day, almost twice as much as lesser establishments, but Clint was glad to pay it.

At the stableman's recommendation, Clint took a nice room in the Cattleman's Hotel. He ordered a bath and sent for a Chinese laundryman to come and take his clothes out to be washed and pressed. He threw away the blood-caked shirt he was wearing. When he had finished his bath, he doctored and rebandaged the nasty bullet wound across his upper arm, pulled a new shirt out of his bag, and then headed off to find a barber shop. He had no trouble locating one and was immediately urged to settle right down for a shave and haircut because the old men already in the shop were just swapping lies and smoking cigars while he was a paying customer.

The barber was a man in his fifties and he was a talker, but Clint was content to just listen to the local news, all about politics and the new silver discoveries around Bisbee and Tombstone.

When the barber finished cutting Clint's hair and had

wiped away all the whiskers and lather, he stared. "By God," he whispered, "I know who you are! You're the Gunsmith!"

Clint rubbed his smooth jaw and nodded with little enthusiasm. He always hoped in vain not to attract any attention. It was better that way because he did not like hero worshipers, autograph seekers, or reputation hunters. "Just as soon you kept that to yourself."

"Too late—these other men heard me. Didn't you, boys?"

The three old-timers had stopped lying to each other and were nodding that they had; suddenly, one of them jumped up and shuffled out. Clint had no doubt it was to spread the word to his friends. "How much do I owe you?"

"Not a damn thing but your autograph and the right to keep the hair clippings, sir."

"Suit yourself." Clint scribbled his name on the barber's towel, then had a change of heart, and did the same for the others who had suddenly managed to find scraps of paper.

"You come to kill anybody?" one of them asked.

"Nope. I am just passing through and seeking a little peace and quiet."

"Look, his arm is bleeding through his shirt!"

Clint glanced at his arm and scowled, thinking about how he had ruined the damn shirt and that it had been one of his favorites.

"What happened?"

"Some Mexican bandits jumped me a few miles north of Nogales. Wasn't much to talk about."

"How many did you kill?"

"Every man I have ever killed was one I wished I had not. But I never had a choice in the matter. Now, where can I find a nice, private saloon where I won't be bothered?"

"O'Ginty's Saloon is the one you want. Sean O'Ginty don't let anybody pester his customers, even the law thinks twice about making an arrest there. Bet you killed at least ten Mexicans, didn't you, Gunsmith?"

The barber looked so eager that Clint nodded wearily. "At least," he said, heading for the door and O'Ginty's Saloon.

The saloon was to his liking. "Mister, I already heard that you are the Gunsmith," Sean O'Ginty said in a thick Irish brogue, "and I have posted one of me boys out by the door to keep out the little people, if you know what I mean."

"Thanks," Clint said, sizing the Irishman up. Sean O'Ginty looked like an ex-pug, he had a fist-busted nose and his brows were prominent with scar tissue. His neck was as big around as Clint's thigh and one ear was bitten half off. He walked with the rolling gait of a sailor or a professional athlete, and his arms were so corded with muscle that they hung out from his sides. Clint figured he could understand full well why even the law did not bother anyone in this saloon.

"What's your favor? Whiskey, beer, rye, champagne? You name it and you'll have my best on the house."

"If I pay for my own drinks," Clint said, "I'm beholden to no man—but then, I can tell that you are not one to keep score, so I'll drink your best beer."

O'Ginty slapped his massive fists together and shouted to the bartender, "Get the Gunsmith some cold beer from down in the cellar, and put a spur up your ass, Dennis!"

Clint had to grin for the order could have been heard from one end of Tucson to the other. Dennis knew it too because he colored with embarrassment, but he did not dare protest, not to Sean O'Ginty.

The beer, true to the promise, was cold and delicious. The saloon owner sat watching him drink it and had one, too. "Why don't you stay for a while?"

Clint wiped suds off his upper lip and frowned. "Why should I stay here when I don't like this damned heat?"

"Hell, man, with a cold beer in your hand and a beautiful woman to love night or day, what could be finer?"

"My gun is not for hire, so what could I possibly do here?"

"Nothing that you haven't done already. Just by being here, choosing my fine establishment to spend your time, you have given me fine publicity. I should like to have a painter do your picture, and then I would hang it over the bar—with your permission and your autograph, of course."

"Of course." Clint chuckled, but when he saw O'Ginty's expression darken, he hastened to add, "I am honored, but no thanks. I am only spending a day or two to rest up and then I'm on my way up north to visit a friend and do some trout fishing."

"God! Would I like to get out of here and go with you!"

"Come along then! The woman I'm going to stay with has a small tourist resort beside a beautiful lake. It's green and cool up there, a bit of old Ireland."

"Heaven, you mean," the man whispered. "Maybe next year. Now, about my offer, all the cold beer or whiskey you can drink, plus food, plus your pick of the most beautiful woman in Tucson."

This time Clint laughed outright. "That's the finest offer I've had in years, but what if I chose a married woman, for example? This isn't worth spilling blood over, Sean."

"No," the big Irishman said, rubbing his jaw. "Let me change that to your choice of unmarried and willing young women."

"No, thank you. I never have needed any help finding women, and I like to think that I can do all right on my own in that respect."

"You might not be aware that we have a beauty or two in Tucson, not the kind that you saw hawking business on the street corners, either."

"I am sure that you do," Clint said. "But all the same, no thanks, I . . ."

"What are you staring at?"

"Her," the Gunsmith said with a low whistle. There had been a curious crowd of men and women in front of the saloon, some peeking over the batwing doors and others through the clean glass window. One had just caught his eye, a beautiful red-headed young woman with rosy cheeks and wide, smiling lips.

"That is Jenny Neal," the saloon owner said without enthusiasm.

"Is she married?"

"No, but . . ."

The girl seemed to be aware that they were watching her, and she flushed with embarrassment and hurried away.

"Now, for a chance to meet her, I might even stay a few extra days for that portrait, Mr. O'Ginty."

The Irishman scowled. "You would pick the toughest one in town. She is not an innocent virgin. No, I don't mean that, but she is . . ."

"Is she married or engaged?"

"No, but . . . listen, Gunsmith, if I can get her to meet you privately, do we have a deal?"

"Just a meeting, a chance to take her to dinner and maybe for a buggy ride some evening. That's all I ask."

"Sure! That's the idea, get her away so that the two of you are all alone! Good idea. I'll do it!"

"All right," Clint said, "we have a deal."

They shook then, with O'Ginty so enthusiastic that he almost crushed the Gunsmith's hand. Twenty minutes later an artist was setting up his easel where a table had been, and the crowd outside was even larger as he quickly began to mix his paints.

Clint sipped his beer, listened to the piano player, and let his heat-punished body relax. This was the craziest deal he had ever gotten himself into, but what the hell, he had liked Sean O'Ginty immediately and the girl was absolutely lovely. Even if nothing came of their meeting, he was a man who appreciated just being near a beautiful girl like that and enjoying her conversation.

The way Clint had it figured, he had absolutely nothing to lose.

THREE

Clint studied himself in the mirror as he shrugged into his freshly washed and pressed coat. He smoothed his hair and then reached over and carefully placed his black Stetson hat on his head. Not bad, he thought, for a man who had ridden across sixty miles of the hellish Arizona desert. He hoped that Jenny Neal found him handsome and that Sean O'Ginty had told her that the Gunsmith wanted to take her out to the nicest dinner establishment in Tucson.

Satisfied with his appearance, Clint locked his room and headed for O'Ginty's Saloon. It was early evening and the temperature was still in the low nineties, down from a scorching one hundred that had left all of Tucson panting and miserable. Clint thought once again of how cool and refreshing it would be up in the mountains. If that Jenny Neal had not captivated him so, he would be on his way out of this desert hell come daybreak; if O'Ginty failed to arrange a date for them, the Gunsmith knew he would be leaving for sure.

O'Ginty's Saloon was packed when he pushed his way inside. The piano player was beating out a rousing tune, and every gambling table except the one that O'Ginty held personal claim to was filled.

"Gunsmith! Top of the evening to you!" the Irishman yelled from behind his bar.

"Same to you, Sean."

"What will you have?"

"A beer."

"Comin' right up!"

Clint moved on back to O'Ginty's private table and settled in. Right close by, the artist was still at work on his canvas, and several men were bold enough to come on back and compare the art with the man who was being portrayed. Clint pretended not to pay them any attention, but when someone said that the painting looked a few years younger and handsomer than its subject, Clint could not help but scowl in anger.

"Well," O'Ginty said, dropping himself into a chair beside Clint, shoving a cool mug of beer in his direction, and then hoisting one of his own, "I must say, Gunsmith, you look the picture of health this evening. Nice suit of clothes."

"Thanks. I want the artist to paint me like this, not dressed in some dusty riding outfit."

"Hear that, Francois? He wants you to paint him wearing this tie and coat, not the way you got it now."

The artist, a slender, nervous, and foppish young man in his early thirties, flew into a rage of French that no one but Sean O'Ginty understood.

"Damn you!" O'Ginty roared, slamming his massive fist down on the table hard enough to set the mugs of beer leaping an inch high, "I don't care what you have to do to change it! Scrape the paint off around his neck and paint in a collar and tie! This is a very famous man and I don't want him looking like a common hand. Make him look dignified, Francois!"

The French artist burst into another tirade, but when O'Ginty started to rise from his chair possibly to rearrange the man's neck, the artist whirled back to his painting and scrapped off the canvas. Then he began to paint in a tie and collar just as pretty as you please.

"I already like that better," Clint said. "Too bad he had to take it so personal."

"Aw, hell," O'Ginty said, "artist's temperament. But he knows the smell of money. This one was so busted he was sketching people on the street with a tin cup at his feet. I gave him honest work. He ought to be grateful and feel privileged to paint the portrait of one as famous as you for my saloon."

Clint hid a smile. He watched the artist mixing his paints, and it was obvious that the man was furious. But he was smart enough to know that he had better keep a grip on himself or O'Ginty would give him a reason to be upset.

"Miss Neal," he said, getting to the topic of his real interest, "was she pleased when you told her that the Gunsmith requested the pleasure of her company?"

O'Ginty's eyes dropped to his big hands. "Well, actually," he hedged, "she . . ."

"I understand," the Gunsmith said, forcing a brave smile, "and that is quite all right. After all, she is obviously of high social standing and it is not the first time that a young lady has denied herself the pleasure of my companionship fearing that it would put her in an unfavorable light. I am, after all, an ex-gunfighter of some reputation, and while that, shall we say, stimulates some women, it makes others fearful."

"But that's not it at all."

"Then what?"

O'Ginty was silent for almost a full minute to the point where Clint was getting angry. The Irishman finally shrugged and said, "Well, in the first place, Miss Neal is a very shy young lady."

"I can be a gentle and patient man," Clint said. "What about the second place you have not yet mentioned?"

The saloon owner's big face screwed up as if what he had to say was almost painful. "In the second place . . .

damn it, Gunsmith, I didn't want to have to tell you this, but Miss Neal has a little stuttering problem."

Clint was amazed. It was the farthest thing from his mind and most unexpected. "Are you sure? How could one so lovely stutter?"

"She just does. Not usually, but when she's excited, it is just terrible."

"Poor, beautiful woman!" Clint shook his head. "Please tell her that one so afflicted has my deepest sympathy but that it would in no way diminish my pleasure in sharing her company for dinner tonight. Knowing what I know, I could not possibly think of seducing one of such a delicate nature."

"Oh, now wait a minute," O'Ginty said, "she is a woman. Been married once already. Her husband died."

The Gunsmith's eyebrows raised. That put an entirely different light on the matter. "In that case, we shall see how the evening goes."

"But what if she still is too shy to have dinner with you tonight?"

On this, Clint was quite firm. "Then our agreement is off. I'll be leaving."

"But what about Francois?"

Clint turned to study the portrait of himself. "He has enough to finish without having me pose any longer. Be honest, O'Ginty, what do you think of it?"

"Looks good to me."

"Do you think it flatters me a little too much? Is too young looking?"

"Hell, no! It's your spitting image, Gunsmith."

"That was what I thought, too," Clint said, relieved that the Irishman agreed. "But I do think Francois has painted a few too many wrinkles at the corners of the eyes and that the jawline should be a little bit stronger."

"You know," O'Ginty said, closing one eye and cocking his head as he studied the canvas, "you may just have something there. I'll speak to Francois about it right—"

Clint grabbed the man's thick forearm. "Wait until tomorrow," he advised. "I think Francois has had enough surprises for one day. Delicate artist's temperament, you know."

O'Ginty slowly nodded. "Maybe you're right. If the little bastard quit, I don't think I could find someone to finish it up for me."

Clint pulled out his watch. "Why don't you and I go see Miss Neal? You can make the introductions and I will take things from there."

"It would be much better if you let me have a word with her alone. You see, her father and mother are very old-fashioned and it might look better since they know me."

"All right," Clint conceded, "we'll do it your way, but if you can't arrange dinner or even a rendezvous tonight, I will be riding out tomorrow at daybreak. It's a tough climb out of this desert up into the mountains, and it will be a lot easier on my horse if it is done before midday."

"Sure," O'Ginty said, looking relieved. "You just sit right here and pose a little while for Francois while I go visit the lovely Miss Neal and see what I can do."

"Fine. Have Dennis send over a little whiskey. I am getting hungry and it will dull my appetite until Miss Neal makes up her mind about dinner tonight."

"I'll do my best," O'Ginty said as he left.

"I'm sure of it," Clint replied. "But if you fail, our deal is off."

"Dennis! Take the Gunsmith a bottle of my finest whiskey and be quick about it!"

"Yes, sir!" the already overworked bartender shouted. "I will get a man right on it, O'Ginty!"

"Don't you be insolent with me, damn you!"

Dennis cowered back against the bar as his employer roared. Sean O'Ginty could be an awesome man when provoked.

O'Ginty's whiskey, like his cool beer, was first class, and Clint settled back and sipped at it as Francois painted with a mad ferocity.

She stutters when especially excited, Clint thought. I have never made love to a stuttering woman. It might be an interesting experience, but he would have to play his cards very carefully. He was not the kind of man to make fun of anyone's shortcomings or problems, and besides, Jenny Neal was a vision of loveliness. With a face and a figure like hers, she did not need to say a word all night.

FOUR

In no time at all, Sean O'Ginty was back, and as he shouldered past his customers toward the rear of the saloon, Clint thought he detected a triumphant smile on the Irishman's lips. The news must be good, Clint thought. He has arranged the date with Miss Jenny Neal. That was good. Clint welcomed the company of a beautiful woman over dinner, even if the woman had a stuttering problem and avoided conversation.

"It is done!" O'Ginty proclaimed.

"That's fine," Clint said, starting to rise out of his chair. "Where shall I . . ."

"Whoa up a minute," the saloon owner said, gently pulling Clint back down in his chair. "There is no hurry. In fact, you'll be happy to know that I have saved you the price of a very expensive dinner."

"What does that mean?"

"Just this. Miss Neal told me that her parents would never understand her going out in public with a man of your reputation."

"But—"

"Let me finish, Clint. But the girl definitely wants to meet you. She thinks you are romantic and very handsome."

"No kidding!"

"No kidding. She is coming up to your room later tonight for a private rendezvous."

"She said that?" Clint rocked back in his chair. The young lady was beautiful!

"Right," Sean responded.

Clint's chest swelled up. "I'll make her glad she came," he promised, feeling a current of excitement. "When can I expect her?"

"Might be pretty late. She has to wait until her parents go to sleep before she can sneak out. You ought to see her, Clint, she is so damned excited she is going to be a wild woman in your bed tonight."

"Whew!" Clint grinned. "I sure am glad I waited, Sean. Nice work."

"Aw, shit," he said, "don't you think a thing about it. Besides, I am doing it for my own best interests, too; I can tell that Francois needs another day or two with you sitting for your portrait, and you are the best advertisement for business that this saloon ever had. My profits are triple what they would be if you weren't my star attraction."

"Then this has worked out to both of our advantages," Clint said.

"Especially yours." The Irishman winked and grinned with lascivious delight. "God, what I wouldn't give to be in your bed tonight!"

Clint laughed. "Tell Francois not to expect me in too early for a sitting. I might need to sleep late."

Clint had eaten a good steak dinner. He had taken a bottle of champagne, compliments of Sean O'Ginty, up to his room and straightened everything up nice for the lady. Then, he had settled back to wait and read the Tucson newspaper. Around eleven o'clock he grew impatient and popped the cork on the champagne and wished that Jenny Neal's parents went to bed a little earlier. By midnight, he was nodding and half asleep. To hell with this, he decided, noticing that the champagne was already half gone. I'll wait for her in bed. That way we can make up for lost time; besides, we won't be able to carry on a conversation anyway, poor lovely girl.

He awoke late in the night as the floor creaked beside his bed. Clint's hand flashed for the gun he had draped over the bedpost. The room was almost totally black, but he felt the hand of Jenny Neal touch his face and then her lips brush across his cheek.

Clint eased his gun back into its holster. "Miss Neal?" he asked groggily, trying to shake the sleep off. "How'd you get in here without knocking?"

"K–k–key."

She laid the key on his chest. "Did the desk clerk give it to you?" he said, placing it on his nightstand and gazing up and wishing he could see her better.

Jenny nodded in the darkness.

Obviously the girl was terrified and afflicted with a frightful case of the nerves, and to reassure and comfort her fears, Clint reached up and gently kissed her lips. "Just try to relax. I am a very gentle man and I have never been selfish in lovemaking. I feel honored that you would come here out of trust, Miss Neal."

In answer, she hugged him fiercely, and now her hand reached under the sheets and went right to his still unawakened manhood. For some reason, Clint was a little amazed and even shocked by this sudden and unexpected boldness. "My, you don't much believe in messin' 'round with the preliminaries, do you?" he said as she flung the covers back and began to nuzzle his chest.

She breathed heavily as she worked lower and lower on him until her tongue was licking his rapidly swelling manhood.

Clint shook his head and then smiled up at the ceiling. It was not often that he read women wrong. At first glance Jenny Neal appeared to be the epitome of innocence, almost to the point of being angelic—but what she was doing to him now told Clint that this was no angel, but instead, a devil! This discovery did not upset him in the least.

And she was good! Maybe her tongue got in her way when she tried to talk, but there was nothing wrong with how it was handling itself right now. Clint swallowed and felt his breath begin to quicken and his hips start to move in time with her as she laved his swollen and eager member. When he could stand it no longer, he reached down and pulled her up to him and then rolled over on top of her. "Miss Neal," he said, "I feel terrible about your losing your husband. Having a wife like you in his bed every night would sure make dying hard to take."

He bent his head to her fine breasts and began to dart his tongue across her nipples. She moaned and began to writhe with pleasure. Her knees bent and her heels rhythmically worked up and down the sheets. After a few minutes, she reached down and grabbed his swollen manhood and crammed it deep into herself. She gasped, arched her hips to his, and then began to buck and yelp as he stroked her long and to the hilt.

Jenny Neal nipped his shoulder and threw her legs around his narrow hips as her body began to jerk out of control. Then Clint was driving deep into her and suddenly they both exploded, mouths locked together, bodies straining and slick with perspiration. Clint completely lost himself in this woman, and it seemed to take five minutes before she drained him of the last of his seed.

When he could catch his breath, he said, "Jenny, that

is as good as I have had in a long time." He started to lift his body from hers, but she tightened her long, silken legs around his waist and began to pump him ever so slowly.

"So," Clint laughed, "you want more real quick, huh?"

"Ye–ye–yeah!" she said.

"Well, you got it all night long," he said, feeling himself stiffening all over again. "This time is going to be a little slower and even better. I got a hunch we are going to have a long and memorable night, you and I."

She giggled, pulled his face to her gorgeous breasts, and shivered when he sucked on her nipples. "Won . . . der . . . ful!" she cooed.

"See," he laughed, "that time you hardly stuttered at all! Hell, by dawn I will have you doing tongue twisters with the best of us."

In answer, she gripped his buttocks fiercely and pulled him in even deeper as if to tell him that she was not really that interested in conversation anyway.

FIVE

Clint slept very, very late, and when he awoke, the sun was beating down on Tucson with an unrelenting ferocity. He reached out for Jenny, but the woman was gone as he had guessed. Clint groaned with contentment. Still half in a dream state, he let his mind relive the wonder and passion of the night before. Jenny Neal was a tiger, a woman of insatiable and thunderous passion. Without question, a lesser man would have folded up his tent and passed out after the fifth or sixth time they made love.

He had claws marks on his back and shoulders, and little red patches where she had nipped the private parts of his body. There was not an inch of him that she did not fully explore. Clint felt as if he had been worked over by a mob of thugs, and yet . . . yet he could not wait until tonight when he and Jenny would do it all over again.

I will have a nap this afternoon, he thought groggily as he rolled out of bed. Yes, I must rest or I won't be up to what she has in mind for us again. Making that promise, he pushed himself out of bed and pulled on his pants, then unlocked his door, and plodded down the hallway toward a room where a Chinaman filled a bath if a person gave him a dime.

The water was cool, not hot, and it felt wonderful. The Chinaman's eyes widened a little when he saw the love marks all over Clint's body. The man said nothing as he poured water over Clint.

He soaked for a full hour, and when he climbed out, he felt like a new man and was totally refreshed. Clint went back to his room, shaved, dressed, and headed for a café where he could get a hearty meal. It was lunch time and he was ravenous because Miss Neal had drained him completely.

He ate well and then headed back to his hotel for a long siesta. By five o'clock he was awake, and the upstairs room was so hot he decided he would go see O'Ginty and have a cool beer and sit awhile for the artist.

Francois was not happy with him. He had probably been waiting for hours, but Clint did not care. He was, however, pleased to see that the portrait had been altered a little and that the lines from the corners of his eyes were gone and that his jawline was a little stronger.

"Nice work, Francois," he said, sipping his beer and easing into his chair. "Why don't you go ahead and finish it up while I drink this?"

Francois' lip curled with contempt and he mumbled something in French that was definitely not complimentary. Clint let it pass. He was in a fine mood and all he could think of was Jenny Neal and tonight.

"Gunsmith!" O'Ginty roared. "How was your little tête-à-tête?"

"My what?"

"Tête-à-tête," O'Ginty repeated. "It is a French word, right, Francois?"

The artist smiled thinly.

O'Ginty explained. "It means a very private meeting between two people."

"It was fine."

"Only fine?"

Clint blushed a little in spite of himself. "Actually,"

he admitted, "it was a night to remember. You ought to see if you can bed her yourself when I leave, Sean. She is unbelievable."

"I had guessed," he said. "You know, she actually killed her poor husband that way."

"You're kidding!"

"Nope. Screwed him into the grave. When she married the poor fella, he was a big strapping man like myself, but each month they were married he got skinnier and skinnier until he was all bones and had bags under the eyes. One night, he just gave it all that he had and it burst his poor heart."

"How do you know?" Clint asked suspiciously.

"Mortician told me privately that all his blood had gone from his heart and brain to where it was needed most."

"You mean to his—"

"That's right," O'Ginty intoned solemnly.

"Sonofabitch," Clint whispered. "After last night, I can believe it!"

"On a regular nightly basis," O'Ginty said, leaning forward to make sure that he was not overheard, "I am afraid that Miss Jenny is fatal."

"But what a way to go, huh, Sean?"

The big Irishman grinned. "It'd almost be worth it, Gunsmith. I believe it really would."

When the heat abated some, Clint finished his third beer and decided that he was hungry again. He went to check on Duke, and when he was satisfied that the big gelding was being well taken care of, he started back toward the town, but then he had an inspiration. Tonight, he would take Miss Neal out for a buggy ride in the moonlight. That would break up the action just a little and it would probably be a real treat for her.

Feeling good about that idea, he paid the liveryman a

silver dollar and ordered the man's finest buggy to be brought around behind the Cattleman's Hotel. Then he strode back to town. There was something about a buggy ride under the stars and making love right out in the open that brought out the best in a man and woman.

It was still in the nineties when he walked down the boardwalk searching for a new café to try. If he looked out at the barren mountains, he could see heat waves dancing over them, and Clint was once again reminded that it was time to leave Tucson and head north where he wanted to spend a relaxing summer. Come fall, he might just return to Tucson and set up shop to gunsmith for the winter. That would really please O'Ginty and it was nice to think of spending some of his free time in the Irishman's saloon where his own portrait hung in a place of honor. And even more pleasant was the thought of taking up again with Miss Neal. If she didn't kill him first, he thought he might even cure her of the stuttering. He remembered how well she had said *wonderful* and knew that he was responsible for her dramatic exclamation.

By damned, he thought with a smile, helping this wonderful woman get over her stuttering was a thing that any man could be proud of and enjoy.

Clint was peering in the windows of the stores and cafés when he reached the sheriff's office. Ordinarily he would not have paid it a lot of attention since his years of being a lawman had convinced him that they all pretty much looked the same. They had old desks all patched up and then given by the city fathers who expected some kind of immense gratitude for donating what they were ashamed of sitting behind themselves; yellowed and fly-specked wanted posters, about half of which were worthless since their outlaws were either hung, shot, or in prison; a rifle rack and a flea-bitten dog sleeping beside the potbellied stove. That was what a sheriff's office looked like. It had all that and iron cells along the back wall, hidden in a separate room if the lawman were lucky.

But this sheriff's office had something so special about it that it stopped Clint in his tracks and made his mouth fall open. It contained four lawmen sitting around and right in their center was none other than Miss Jenny Neal!

Clint stared for a minute and then stumbled on. Seeing Miss Neal in daylight again made him realize all over what an extraordinary beauty she was and how lucky he had been and would be for the second night in a row.

Clint stopped a few doors down. He believed that she had green eyes. He wasn't certain. He wanted to see her if only for a moment, so he waited. What was she doing in the sheriff's office? Was she in trouble and too proud to tell him? Clint resolved to buy a paper and pencil, and if she couldn't tell him, then at least he could determine whether she needed help.

He had to wait almost a quarter of an hour, but finally she emerged and started in his direction.

She was frowning, lost in concentration, but Clint was in awe of how fresh and radiant she appeared, not even the hint of a dark circle under lovely—yes, green!—under her lovely green eyes.

"Afternoon, Jenny," he said as she walked by. He fell in beside her. "How are you feeling after what we did together all last night?"

She looked up at him quickly and then began to walk faster.

"I rented us a buggy. We are going to go out and make love under the stars."

The girl paled and began to run.

"What's the matter? Look, I'm sorry. I guess you're

worried about being seen with me, but I just had to ask if you were in some kind of trouble or . . . Stop a minute, Jenny!"

He grabbed her arm and that is when she threw back that beautiful head of hers and screamed. "Help! Somebody help me, please!"

"Your stutter, Jenny, you lost your stutter!"

"Help! Call the sheriff!"

"It's a miracle that it is all gone! I don't—"

Suddenly, a man shouted, "Jenny, drop to the ground!"

The girl fell as if she had been poleaxed, and as Clint twisted around, he stared in horror as the sheriff and his deputies opened fire.

"Wait, there's been a—"

Clint felt hot lead whipping past his face and knew that there was no time for an explanation. Someone had made a terrible mistake, and he figured that someone was that sneaky, tricky sonofabitch of an Irishman who had sent him a ringer last night. The real Jenny Neal was screaming her pretty head off and she damn sure was no stutterer.

"O'Ginty," Clint roared, "when we meet, you are a dead man!"

And then he ducked into an alley and started to run. He was going to find that overgrown, deceitful Irishman. All deals between them were now off, and the Gunsmith figured it was time to settle the score.

SIX

They were after him and Clint knew that they were not interested in hearing explanations, especially one as crazy as his. Now, as he sprinted down the alley, it occurred to him that he needed to get to his hotel room, grab his rifle and belongings, and then clear out of town fast.

He was running in the right direction, but as he looked back, he saw the lawmen burst into the alley, guns blazing. They were still at least fifty yards behind but were coming fast. Clint heard a bullet buzz past his ear and then another clipped his heel. The alley was long and straight, and the way he figured it, the odds were that a bullet would bring him down before he reached the rear of the hotel.

Clint dodged into the first side street, and for a minute, he knew he was out of the sight of his pursuers. His chest was heaving and his lungs were on fire. A man wasn't meant to run this furiously and Clint was not accustomed to running from anyone. Now, he thought, remembering all the wanted men he had hunted down and captured, I understand how they felt.

The side alley was dark and it was filled with garbage cans and water barrels. Clint shook every one he passed until he felt one of the water barrels rock easily, its water sloshing only at its lower few inches. Glancing back toward the alley, he calculated he had about ten seconds to get into the barrel, and somehow he made it.

The barrel was moss-covered and slimy inside, and he

did not appreciate what it was doing to his clean suit, not to mention his polished boots. But when he heard the racing footsteps pounding by, Clint forgot all about his clothes, and with his Stetson in one hand and his gun in the other, he felt almighty grateful just to be in one piece still.

"You men, check Main Street in both directions. Ask everyone where that bastard went, and when you find him, take him dead or alive!"

"Where are you going?"

"To the Cattleman, just in case he's stupid enough to try to pick up his belongings before making his escape! Phil, you come with me! Ed, you find the stable where he is boarding that horse he rode in on. He won't want to leave an animal like that behind."

Clint cussed out loud in that water barrel. The sheriff was a good lawman, and he was under control, thinking and doing everything according to the book. If you took a man's outfit and his horse away, he probably wasn't going to get very far, very fast.

"That does it," Clint said. "There is only one way out of this stupid mess and that is to find Sean O'Ginty and make him tell the truth!"

He eased out of the water barrel with moss and slime all over him. "Damn it!" he growled, shucking out of his coat and pitching it back into the barrel as he replaced his Stetson and quickly moved back the way he had come.

Every saloon that Clint had ever been in had a front and a back door. Now, as Clint hurried down the alley, he guessed he would choose the latter. But when he reached it, it was locked. Clint had to work hard to avoid shooting the damned door open. Instead, he reversed his gun and pounded on the door.

"Go away," said someone who sounded like the young bartender named Dennis. "You want a drink, go through the front door like a civilized man!"

"Let me in, Dennis! This is the Gunsmith!"

"They are searching the town for you!"

"I know." Clint pounded the door. "That's why I need you to let me in!"

"Maybe I should ask Sean first," came the worried reply.

"You let me in this way or when I come in the front door, you are going to eat the barrel of my gun, damn it!"

Dennis decided to let him in. When the door swung open, Clint found he was in a supply room with cases of liquor and barrels of beer. "Where's O'Ginty?"

"Tending bar while I . . ."

Clint wasn't interested in hearing the rest of the story. He swept past the young man and charged across the supply room.

"Please, don't tell him that I . . ."

Clint eased open the rear door that led into the saloon and peered inside. O'Ginty's was almost empty. Through the front pane windows, he could see men running up and down the boardwalk out front and he guessed that everyone was in a big lather about his being hunted by the sheriff and his deputies for molesting a decent woman. And the woman he had thought was Jenny Neal was decent. Too bad she was not the woman he had made love to the night before.

O'Ginty had taken the momentary lull in business to clear the back wall of his bar for the Gunsmith's oil portrait, which was not completely dry yet. The Irishman had hired someone to make a gilded frame and now he was admiring it fondly.

Clint put a finger to his lips and motioned Dennis to keep quiet and be still; he wanted to hear what O'Ginty had to say to his patrons and he was as safe as possible where he stood. He heard O'Ginty proclaim to one of the customers, "Men are going to die out there in our streets today. The Gunsmith won't be taken to jail alive. Four against his one, I'd say that was about even odds."

"Ten bucks says Sheriff John Rankin or one of his deputies nails the bastard!"

"You are on!" O'Ginty cried. "I'll take even money that, when the smoke clears, it'll be the Gunsmith who waltzes through the door and orders drinks on the house for his friends."

A heavyset man in his late fifties crashed through the front doors. He was rumpled, coated with dust, and out of breath. By the cut and look of his derby and clothes, he was easily pegged as an easterner, and one of some means as evidenced by the long cigar clenched between his teeth and the massive watch chain he wore across his protruding silk vest. As he waved his hands and tried to catch his breath, diamonds sparkled on both of his pinky fingers.

"O'Ginty, I heard that and I must say you give poor odds. Everyone knows the Gunsmith is equal to five ordinary guns. However, give me two-to-one that the Gunsmith walks through that door alive and I will wager you one thousand dollars!"

The Irishman did not like to be told that his odds were stingy, especially in his own saloon. "Who the blazes are you?" he growled.

"Oscar Marsh, better known out West as the Legend Maker. I am sure you have heard of me."

"Hell, no!"

The easterner did not seem bothered at all by what he

obviously considered the man's ignorance. "I am, gentlemen, the sole owner, proprietor, and promoter of the Great Wild West Outlaws and Gunfighters Show!"

Clint smiled with cold amusement. He had heard rumors and was curious enough to want to hear just a little more.

"The Great Wild West Outlaws and Gunfighters Show?" O'Ginty was not impressed. "What the hell is that?"

"It is, gentlemen, the greatest traveling show and assemblage of legends ever gathered under one roof! I, Oscar Marsh, have under contract the great—and soon to be greater—western legends of our time. We book and tour the largest eastern cities and pack the houses as my gunfighters and outlaws stage mock gunfights and battles, and, then, in their own immortal words, tell movingly of the carnage they have wrought to mankind by their savagery."

"Hmmm," O'Ginty said, "sounds interesting."

"Interesting? Interesting!" Oscar Marsh threw his head back and yelled, "It is grand entertainment!"

"Who you got under your tent right now, Mr. Marsh?"

The promoter was obviously caught off guard by the question.

"Well, at the moment, I have none other than Jake Bosco, and let me tell you, I am ensuring him a place in history! History!"

"Never heard of the man," O'Ginty said.

"Who the hell is Jake Bosco?" someone asked.

Clint had heard enough. The Legend Maker, as he called himself, was nothing but a self-promoting purveyor of lies about the west. There were dozens of such opportunists roaming about, eager to profit from the life and times of anyone who ever drew a gun and lived to tell the story. Clint had already had his experience with a money-hungry dime novelist who used his name and legend for profit, and this man appeared to be exactly the same type of character.

Clint figured it was time to set the record straight about poor Jake Bosco, about himself, and about Miss Jenny Neal.

SEVEN

Moving into the saloon, watching heads turn, and noting the astonishment his entrance caused, Clint said, "Jake Bosco must indeed be a hell of an attraction, Oscar, because he has been dead for three months. Before you got hold of him, he was nothing but a poor Missouri pig farmer who took up ambushing carpetbaggers until one of them lived to shoot back at him. Bosco was found hiding in his pig pen three months ago and shot down with his sows who promptly ate him before the mortician arrived."

"As I live and breathe, it is none other than the Gunsmith himself!" the easterner cried, entirely ignoring what had just been revealed. "A legend all the people of our mighty eastern cities wait to see and hear in person as the star attraction of my Great Outlaws and Gunfighters Show!"

"Not interesed in the least," Clint said as he moved down the bar toward Sean O'Ginty, who was just now beginning to recover. "Anyone leaves this room before me is asking for a bullet."

O'Ginty placed the oil portrait on the bar and somehow managed a grin. "Look at this, my famous friend. Francois has created a work of art almost worthy of you! And see how I've had it framed—in gold, Gunsmith! In gold! Aren't you pleased? It will be a great tribute to your name!"

Clint reached out for the portrait and studied it closely. Francois had done a masterful job all right. It flattered him a little, but not in excess.

O'Ginty nervously tugged at the tips of his waxed mustache. "What do you think?"

Clint lifted the portrait and brought it crashing down on the Irishman's head. The canvas split. O'Ginty's thick skull punched through as the gilded frame slammed down over his powerful shoulders, momentarily pinning his arms to his sides. Clint reared back and sent every ounce of muscle he possessed into a thundering blow that caught O'Ginty square on his paint-smeared nose and sent him crashing back into his wall of bottles.

"That's what I think," Clint shouted, heading around the bar and coming at the Irishman with murder in his eyes. It was time to administer a beating and a lesson before he dragged the man outside and got this mess straightened out.

O'Ginty had not risen to his present stature as owner of Tucson's finest saloon because he was soft and easy. He was a two-fisted brawler of some reputation and owned a murderous punch. Now, as Clint bore in on him, he lifted the ruined portrait, stared at it for a moment, and then roared, "You've cost me a hundred dollars. Damn you, Gunsmith!"

Clint did not care. While the powerful man's eyes were still a little glassy from his best punch, he meant to take advantage and teach the saloon owner a lesson. He sent a straight left to O'Ginty's right eye that staggered the man, and then he followed it with a booming uppercut to his massive jaw. O'Ginty dropped to his knees.

"Get up," Clint said. "You tricked me into staying and now I am wanted by the law. They are trying to shoot me!"

O'Ginty lunged from a crouch and his powerful arms locked around Clint's knees. They both went down kicking and punching behind the bar as the patrons shouted and started making bets as to who would win.

Clint took a bone-crushing blow on the jaw that caused lights to blossom behind his eyes, and dimly he heard the odds swing heavily into O'Ginty's favor; they sounded about right to him, O'Ginty was bigger, stronger, and every bit as determined to win.

The Irishman managed to get on top, and he sledged a fist down at Clint's face but missed when Clint swung his head sideways. The fist smashed into the floor and O'Ginty howled. Clint grabbed a bottle of imported brandy and cracked it over the bigger man's skull. The bottle shattered and fiery liquor poured down into his face, but O'Ginty slumped and Clint rolled free, then pulled himself erect, and panted, "Get up. We're not finished."

O'Ginty groaned, shook his head, and stared up at Clint. "I can't have you using my finest liquor to break over my skull. Use the cheap stuff, damn it!"

Clint waited for the saloon owner to rise to his knees and then he belted him solidly. The Irishman crashed over backward, but amazingly he started to get up again.

"You deceived me," Clint said, suddenly tired of fighting and deciding that O'Ginty had been punished enough. "And now you are going out there to find the sheriff and get this misunderstanding cleared up before someone gets killed."

"Such as yourself?" O'Ginty said, climbing back to his feet and wiping blood from a split lip.

"That's right. You're the only one who can get this mess straightened out. All I did was assume that the girl coming out of the sheriff's office was Miss Neal."

"What did you say to her?"

"I told her I liked how she . . . well, you know."

O'Ginty groaned and that made Clint even angrier.

"Well, how was I to know? Who was she anyway?" Clint asked.

"That really is Miss Neal. She happens to be engaged to our sheriff."

Now Clint understood why the man had reacted as he had. "Explain things to him!"

"The sheriff, he won't understand." O'Ginty sighed helplessly.

"Make him! You owe me that much."

"I owe you nothing anymore. Not after what you did with that painting I paid for!"

Clint seriously debated whether or not he should just shoot this conniving sonofabuck or what. But if he did, there went his explanation and he would then have to face down the sheriff.

"Listen," Clint said, "if you smooth this out, I'll come back this fall and pose for another portrait."

"You mean that?"

"Word of honor."

Oscar Marsh piped in. "When a famous gunfighter gives you his word of honor, he—"

"Oh, shut up!" O'Ginty roared. He glared at Clint. "All right, we got a deal. Shake."

They shook. O'Ginty used a wet bar rag to clean the smeared paint and blood from his face and then he glared at the easterner. "Oscar, if you ever write his story, you better tell what just happened here and how I'd have whipped him if he hadn't used that expensive bottle of brandy across my skull."

"Winners win," the easterner said coldly.

Before O'Ginty reached for the fat promoter's throat, Clint moved between them, saying, "Get out there and find the sheriff before he finds me and the bullets start flying."

O'Ginty nodded, stared at the punctured canvas, and

shook his head sadly. "It would kill poor Francois to see what became of his masterpiece."

"Send for him this fall," Clint said. "Tell him there's another hundred bucks in it for him. That ought to make him happy."

"The hundred bucks was for the framing and the picture frame itself. Francois only got twenty."

Clint bit his tongue and said nothing as the Irishman bulled his way outside to find the sheriff.

"I'd like to buy you a drink," Oscar Marsh said, patting Clint on the back. "I don't yet understand what happened, but I'd like to find out."

"Not for sale, Oscar."

"But that's exactly the kind of stuff that my audiences crave! Danger, romance. That's what brings them to the shows, Gunsmith. They love to know about the personal lives of all my stars." He raised his flabby arm and motioned vigorously. "Bartender, whatever the Gunsmith wants, I'll have the same."

Clint did not object. His face was half-numb and he had taken a rib-bruising punch that he knew would keep him walking and riding a little bent over for days. He wiped his face and tasted the sticky brandy. "Dennis, I'll have a shot of whatever kind of brandy it was that I used on your boss's head."

The bartender flashed him a happy grin. "Yes, sir! A pleasure." It was clear that Dennis was delighted to have seen his boss clubbed with a bottle of his own expensive brandy.

Oscar Marsh waited until the drinks were poured, and then he touched his glass to the Gunsmith's and said, "Here's to a great partnership, my friend. I know you are already famous in the west, but this is very different—you are still a handsome man, one who would have a tremendous personal appeal to the masses.

Listen, after we go on tour, you will be legendary throughout the world.''

''Not interested.''

''At a hundred dollars a week guaranteed.''

''Still not interested.''

Oscar blinked, mopped his sweaty face, and then forced a brave smile. ''I don't believe I heard you right.''

''Sure you did,'' Clint said, tossing his brandy down and pouring another to the brim. ''I said I was not interested.''

Now Oscar Marsh finished his brandy and poured himself another stiff one. ''Perhaps you don't fully understand what I am offering you.''

''The chance to make a lot of money, go on an eastern, possibly even a world tour like Buffalo Bill Cody—only I'd have to shoot targets like a carnival showman. Isn't that true?''

''Well, Gunsmith, no one can make you do all those things. The content of your speech and the nature of your act is somewhat flexible. I would, of course, assist you, but the final say would be entirely of your choosing.''

''I choose to stay the hell off your stage, Oscar. That's as plain as I can put it.''

''I don't understand you at all! Jake Bosco was overjoyed—''

''I knew poor Jake,'' Clint interrupted. ''He was a simple man who hated the Union for what it did to the south, and so he bushwhacked any northern sympathizer he thought would not be a danger to himself. Of course, he wanted you to make him a legend—small men crave fame.''

''But I—''

They were interrupted by O'Ginty banging through

the front doors. "It's settled, Gunsmith."

Clint pushed away from the bar. "You explained everything?"

"Completely. When the sheriff and his deputies heard the full story, they thought it was funny as hell!" O'Ginty laughed.

"Well," Oscar Marsh said, "I guess that calls for drinks on the house."

"Put your money back, Oscar. Sean O'Ginty is buying."

"I am?"

Clint nodded. He took his drink, raised it up to his audience, and said, "To honest men and honest women—and to anonymity."

The Legend Maker frowned, but he showed he had no hard feelings because he drank the toast and then said, "It has been an honor meeting you, Gunsmith. I hope some day we might meet again, and if you should ever change—"

"I won't, but thanks for the offer."

He set his empty glass down and started for the door. He wanted to see the sheriff and then he wanted to get the hell out of Tucson.

He knocked on the sheriff's door and a voice boomed, "Come on in."

Clint opened the door and walked inside to discover himself facing four unwavering guns—no, five—the sheriff was covering him with a double-barreled shotgun. "What—"

"Freeze or we blow you to pieces," the sheriff hissed.

Clint froze. There was just no way that he could win and there had to be some misunderstanding here. "Didn't O'Ginty explain things to you?"

"Yeah, he said you saw my fiancée, Miss Neal, once

and you could not get her out of your filthy mind. You are under arrest, Gunsmith."

"What are the charges?"

"Molesting a decent and respectable woman on the city streets. That's enough to get you sent to prison."

"I am innocent!"

"No, you aren't. Miss Neal will testify as to the foul words you said to her, how you grievously wronged her character."

"I used no foul words at all! What I said was—"

"Don't say a word! Just lift your hands up from your gun and keep your mouth shut. Boys, take his gun. Search him for any other weapons and lock him up."

"I want to see that damned O'Ginty!" Clint swore, letting the deputies take his gun and pat him down. Then they led him to the rear of the office and through a door to a stout iron cell.

"You can see him in court," the sheriff growled.

They shoved him in hard and Clint swung around ready to fight again, but the iron bars shut with a final, metallic ring.

Clint gripped the bars and swore to himself that somehow, someway, he was going to clear his name and his reputation of this terrible smear. Then he was going to get even with Sean O'Ginty—and this time, he wouldn't use his fists. He would use a gun.

EIGHT

He had been inside the jail for a week, and it was obvious to Clint that the sheriff had ordered his deputies to see that he was starved and weakened. Always lean and without fat, Clint now felt that he was starting to lose some muscle. He tried to exercise at first, but when it became apparent that his bread and water diet was not going to be supplemented with substantial food, he decided that he had best conserve every ounce of his energy. Besides the lack of decent food, he was not allowed a wash basin, his razor blade, or a clean change of clothes. Daily, he found that he was slipping deeper into a state of despair, and as yet, they had not told him when he was due to be tried before a federal judge.

It was late afternoon when his first visitor arrived, and when Clint rolled over, he found himself staring at the easterner who called himself the Legend Maker. Clint didn't smile. He looked away. He could well imagine how disreputable he looked, like a common criminal.

Oscar Marsh pursed his smallish lips together and shook his head sympathetically. "I am sorry I didn't come to visit earlier, but the sheriff wouldn't allow it. Are you well?"

"I am being starved," Clint said grimly. "You want to write that?"

"No, no, I do not." Oscar moved forward until he stood beside the bars. He gripped them in his fat hands and stared at Clint. "The sheriff has agreed to allow me to visit."

"You are wasting your time."

"Gunsmith, maybe I can help."

"I don't need your help."

"It appears that you do."

"Why don't you go back east," Clint said wearily.

"Not without your story. You need me, Gunsmith, and I need you."

Clint rolled over to stare at the man. He did not like him, hadn't from the first moment he had laid eyes on him at O'Ginty's Saloon. Oscar Marsh was a parasite. He preyed on men and did not care in the slightest what happened to them after he made them famous. It was obvious that he did not give a damn if the grand reputations that made him his money caused the death of whoever he had immortalized.

"I don't need you," Clint said, closing his eyes and wishing that the man had not come.

Oscar shook the bars in a violent fit of temper. "Don't be a fool! If you help me, I'll help you! I'll hire a decent lawyer. Find some way to get you off scot-free."

Clint sat up. "I'm listening, but unless O'Ginty is willing to come forth and tell the whole story, I don't see how I can beat this one."

"O'Ginty can be bought to say whatever we want him to say."

"All he has to do is tell the truth. Nothing else, just the damn truth!" Clint lowered his voice, realizing that he was nearing the verge of losing control.

"He won't do it without money, and I won't pay him a cent unless you agree to star in my show."

"A little blackmail?"

Oscar smiled. "You call it whatever you want. What is abundantly clear is that you are in deep, deep trouble and I am your only hope. You sign a touring contract or else you won't have a chance in court and your next stop is prison."

Clint weighed the proposition carefully. In all his years as a lawman, it was his experience that ninety percent of the guilty ones still pleaded their innocence even after sentencing. Judges and juries knew that. So, when a man pleaded innocent, it meant nothing. The few who were really innocent were often wrongly sentenced to prison, even the gallows. The law did err, but generally speaking, those errors were rare.

"I am still going to take my chances on the law and our court system," Clint said.

"You are a fool!"

"Maybe, but if there wasn't a set of bars between us, it would be you who was the fool and would be eating his teeth. I'll tell you right out, Oscar, I've had men like you approach me before for my story and the answer has always been the same—no. But I've never met one as cold and calculating as you. Now, get out of here!"

The eastern promoter and showman managed a thin smile. "I am going to tell you something, Gunsmith. When I first learned you were passing through town, I was on my way from Phoenix to El Paso. I ordered the coach to stop and turn around, and when it would not, I let it take me to the first stop. Then I hired the manager and paid him enough to abandon his post and to take the stage horses and get me here to Tucson as fast as those animals could pull a carriage across the damned desert. We killed two, but I reached Tucson in time. Cost me about three hundred dollars, but that is nothing compared to what we can make on a tour together."

"You wasted a lot of money for nothing."

"I don't think so. What have you been up to the last couple of years?"

"Working as a gunsmith."

"That all?"

"I have been in a few tight fixes."

Oscar smiled. "Of course, you have. Men of the gun always do manage to attract others like themselves, and inevitably, blood is spilled. I want to know about those men."

"Get out," Clint said, rising to his feet and moving toward the cell bars.

Oscar edged away and out of reach. "If you go to prison—which you surely will—the newspapers will get hold of the story, and they'll crucify you, Gunsmith. Nobody likes a man who spits on womanhood, insults a lady. All the good you have done over the years will mean absolutely nothing. Your name will be smeared with mud."

"I didn't know Miss Neal was respectable and a lady! I had no reason to suspect she was not the woman I had made love to the night before."

Oscar grinned, pulled a cigar out of his pocket, and lit it before speaking. "I believe you; I believe you. But the judge won't."

Clint sagged with defeat. "I know that. The only man who can get me clear of this mess is Sean O'Ginty, and I can't for the life of me figure out why the big bastard won't just explain things."

"He is afraid of the sheriff. That seems obvious."

"Maybe so," Clint said tiredly.

"I can fix things," Oscar said again. "Just say the word and start talking. When we get an act roughed out, then I'll gladly hire that attorney and pay O'Ginty whatever it takes to make him confess to his deception."

Clint's eyes narrowed. "An honorable man would

do those things without strings, and if you had offered to help without them, I would have given you your damned story—but not like this, not blackmail. Uh-uh, Oscar, I'll just take my chances in court."

The easterner stared at him with a mixture of contempt and pity. "You really are a fool. First man I have come across who neither wanted fame nor would take the obvious and the easy way out of a fix."

"Let me be."

"Has it occurred to you that you might not be alive when the date of your court appearance comes around?"

"Yeah," Clint said, moving wearily back to his thin straw mattress. "That thought crosses my mind about three times a day when I ought to be getting something to eat besides bread and water."

"Sheriff John Rankin is not the kind of man who is kind or merciful to his prisoners."

"So I gather."

"But," Marsh declared solemnly, "I fear that none of the former prisoners who have inhabited the cell you are now in were ever subjected to the fate you must endure. Sheriff Rankin is insanely jealous, and you have insulted his fiancée and that . . . that is absolutely unforgivable."

Clint said nothing because he had about figured this out the same way. It had to be the reason he was being starved.

"I think," Marsh said, dropping his voice to a whisper, "no, I know that you will never reach the courtroom alive."

"Rankin say that to you?" Clint asked.

"Of course not. The man is no fool. My guess is that he will shoot you dead and then contend that you tried to escape. The matter will be swept under the table and no one will know the difference."

"So, if you are so certain that I am a dead man, why are you still trying to work a deal?"

"What good," Marsh asked with a wave of his pudgy fist and cigar, "is a dead legend?"

Clint ran his fingers through his hair. "I still say that an honest judge will see the truth of the thing and that the sheriff, no matter how much he might hate me out of jealousy, will not dare to kill me."

"And you are willing to bet your life on it?"

"That's right," Clint said stubbornly. "And when I reach the courtroom, I will find a way to punch holes in O'Ginty's story and make him tell the truth."

"If you really believe that, Gunsmith, then you are a dead man."

Clint lay back down on his mattress and closed his eyes. "Get out of here, Oscar, the place stinks bad enough as it is."

NINE

"Gunsmith!"

Clint sat up in the dark. It was his tenth day in the cell and despite every threat he could think of, he was still on bread and water and no trial date had been set.

"Oscar?"

The eastern promoter snorted, "Who else gives a damn whether you make it out of this scrape alive or dead? I have some bad news for you."

"Why don't you ask the law to come inside and tell me face to face instead of creeping around in the alley late at night?"

"Because the sheriff figures I am a nuisance. I have demanded over and over that he feed you better. I even offered to pay for it myself."

"I appreciate that." The Gunsmith was feeling too low to generate much appreciation.

"It is a cost of business. You starve to death, there goes my main star for next season."

"I still—"

"I know," Oscar said roughly, "your answer is still no. But you'll change your mind. Listen, I have an idea for a mock gunfight between you and—"

"Damn it, Oscar, what is the news?"

There was a long, injured silence. "All right. The good news is that Judge Wilson is going to hear your case tomorrow."

"But I haven't even seen a lawyer!"

"That is not the bad news, Gunsmith. You ready for the real bad news?"

Clint sighed. "All right, let's get this over with. What is the bad news?"

"The bad news is that along about midnight someone is going to open your cell door and bang around to wake you up. You are supposed to make a run for it, but you won't get five steps out the front door before you are riddled by the sheriff and his deputies."

"It figures," Clint said. "So I'll just stay here and take my chances in the court without an attorney. I have been to enough of these things to know how to plead my own case. But thanks, Oscar. Thanks for the warning."

"So you owe me one, right?"

"Not enough to go on stage like your trained dog or pony act."

"You are a hard sonofabitch, Gunsmith! If you were not so much in demand back east, I would not bother with you at all. Anyway, good luck in court. If you get sentenced to the state penitentiary, I'll have to start all over looking for another main attraction."

"I wish I could work up more sympathy," Clint said, stretching back out on his mattress and closing his eyes to wait, "but I just can't quite do it."

Clint did not go to sleep but lay thinking about what a mess he had gotten himself into. He had no one except himself to blame for trusting big Sean O'Ginty. However, Clint figured that O'Ginty hadn't intended this to go so far. Surely the man could not have seen that the Gunsmith and the real Miss Jenny Neal would happen to meet.

So, it had all been an accident. Fate had conspired to deal him a bad hand of cards. Tomorrow, he would play out the hand in the Tucson courtroom, and he hoped that he would walk away with his chips in his hands.

Maybe when Miss Neal understood what had happened and why he had said to her what he did, she would forgive him and drop the charges.

I would if I were her, Clint thought. It is not fair to send a man to prison just for what I did. But then, life was never fair.

Clint's experience told him that whether a man was honest or dishonest, good or bad, luck seemed to play almost as much importance in where he got in life as anything else. Luck, yeah, and maybe hard work—although the poorest men he had ever met were often the ones with stooped shoulders and calluses on their hands. How many times had he seen honest and hard-working men who had done the right things and labored like mules all their lives end up broke and bitter? One hell of a lot of times.

Some men thought that a man could control his luck and maybe that was true to a certain extent. Clint figured it was more a case of setting things up so the odds were in your favor rather than in someone else's. In his own case, the odds were all set up against him in the courtroom. A judge would almost always rule in favor of the local law officials. A judge and a sheriff, well, they needed each other too much to be fighting and wrangling over cases—they were like a team of horses hitched together. That was to the good, except when either one of them was being vindictive or just plain unreasonable like in this case.

I will call O'Ginty in, Clint thought, and I will sweat him out on the witness stand if I have to. Then when Miss Neal hears him confess what he did to me, she will relent and drop charges. Then, I will settle up with O'Ginty and ride the hell out of this town and never look back.

That was his plan. It made him feel better until he heard the key in his cell door and then listened to the hinges squeak as the door was pushed open. Clint remained motionless and pretended to be asleep.

He heard a lawman's bootheels thumping loudly on the wooden floor and when he still did not stir the man picked up a cuspidor and dropped it on the floor making enough racket to wake a dead man.

Clint did not move a muscle.

"Sonofabitch," Sheriff John Rankin swore. He picked up the cuspidor and hurled it at the cell. The impact rattled the bars and sent Clint an inch off his back, but he settled right down again and pretended to snore.

"Sonofabitch!"

The front door slammed shut and Clint heard the man stomping out across the boardwalk. He opened his eyes and stared up at the black ceiling. Then his shoulders began to shake and he began laughing in the night.

How stupid, he wondered, does that jealous idiot think I am?

The next morning he awoke and the cell door was locked again. Sheriff Rankin was studying him with a look of unconcealed hatred. Rankin was too young to be the sheriff of a town the size of Tucson. A man needed to be at least thirty before he learned to handle the authority that went with the badge; after forty, his reflexes were going to slow down just enough that he might not be able to handle a gun fast enough to stay alive. So thirty to forty was the prime age; to be sheriff at a younger or older age took an exceptional man.

Clint guessed Rankin was only about twenty-five,

twenty-seven tops. He had long brown hair and wore it parted in the center. He was of average height, blocky and square-jawed. Clint had to admit that the man was ruggedly handsome. His eyes were blue and his nose straight; Rankin moved with a cocky arrogance and a grace that was not practiced. He wore two guns, butts facing forward for the cross draw, and Clint supposed he was probably damned fast with either. In the long, heat-punishing days during which Clint had been observing this office, it was clear that the other deputies feared more than respected him. John Rankin was not only insanely jealous, but he had a murderous temper. Two nights ago, he had pistol-whipped a belligerent drunk into unconsciousness, and it had taken all a doctor's skills to save the poor man's life.

"You sleep like the dead!" Rankin said between clenched teeth as he moved to the cell door.

Clint stood up. "I understand we are going to trial today."

"Who told you that?"

"A little bird. How about sending a man to my room at the Cattleman's Hotel and have him bring back a change of clothes and my razor?"

"Not a chance."

"A man deserves to be clean if he chooses!"

Clint's anger obviously amused the sheriff. "So, finally starting to crack are you? Where is that smug grin you wore coming in here? Let me tell you something, Gunsmith. I have heard of your reputation, and as far as I am concerned, you are definitely overrated."

Clint said nothing. Goad this man, Clint thought, and he just might go crazy and kill me right in the cell and then fabricate some escape story.

"What is the matter? Have I told it right? Hell, yes, I

have!'' He turned to his deputies. ''Look at the famous Gunsmith now! Dirty, stinking, and so weak he shakes when he stands. This is a western legend?''

They all began to laugh and Clint had to stand there and just take their abuse. But somehow, things were going to come out even. They always did in cases like this when some arrogant, power-crazed ass like Rankin temporarily got the upper hand. What the Gunsmith had learned over the years was that you had to wait until it was your turn to strike back. You had to wait, no matter how much it hurt your pride, cut it to the bone. And it was very true that the deeper the injustice, the sweeter the revenge.

''Sit down!'' Rankin hissed. ''We leave for the courtroom a quarter to ten, and I wish there was a wind outside so we could stay on the upwind side of you.''

Clint sat. He clenched his hands together until his knuckles were white, and he fought to keep his teeth locked together as his eyes riveted on the clock.

He remained motionless for almost two hours, and then Rankin finally kicked his heels off his desk, found a pair of handcuffs, and came to get him. ''Turn around and put your hands behind your back.''

Clint did as he was ordered. He felt the manacles clamp over his wrists, and then a powerful blow to the kidneys dropped him to his knees. He choked and tried not to pass out.

''Get up,'' the sheriff hissed, dragging him to his feet and shoving him toward the door and into the office where his deputies grabbed him and hustled him outside.

It was already hot, but Clint did not notice as they started him across the street toward the courthouse. A big crowd of people was lined up along the way, and

some of them taunted him, called him a lusting devil
who was finally getting what he deserved.

The Gunsmith lifted his head high and stared straight
ahead, blocking these people from his sight and his
mind. He was no saint, but he had never injured or
shamed or taken advantage of a woman in his life. Not
many men could say that. Clint was not ashamed of a
single damned thing. And he was sure that when he
walked back across this street, it would be as a vin-
dicated and free man.

TEN

The courtroom felt like a furnace when he stepped inside. Every chair and row of seats in the building was filled with gaping spectators, and Clint saw the looks of amazement on their faces when they realized that the shabby, unshaven, and shuffling prisoner being led forward was the Gunsmith. Men he recognized from O'Ginty's Saloon seemed hardly able to believe their eyes.

Clint was led to the front of the courtroom and yanked down hard in his seat. He studied the courtroom with indifference because, like sheriff's offices, they differed little from one another. This one had oaken pews for the spectators. Behind the pews on both sides were stone walls and high up on each were big open windows that he supposed were there to catch an errant breeze, only there was none; it was so stuffy and the air was so dead that even the flies droned slowly.

In the center of the courtroom was a wooden railing beyond which, on a raised platform, was a oak desk for the judge to preside from. To one side was a smaller desk for the court reporter who sat nervously sharpening his pencil.

Satisfied that this room held no surprises, Clint closed his eyes and listened to the murmurs and hushed whispering, and finally, he heard a gavel bang on wood. He looked up to see that Judge Wilson was a very pale man in his sixties with unforgiving features and a pair of spectacles perched on a sharp, hooked nose.

"Hear ye! Hear ye!" the bailiff intoned. "Everyone

57

rise, for this honorable court is now in session and being presided over by the Honorable Judge Harold B. Wilson. God bless this court and these United States of America!"

The judge bowed slightly and then sat. It was the signal for everyone else to be seated as well.

Clint understood perfectly, but Sheriff Rankin took no chances and yanked him down hard, the manacles cutting into his wrists.

Judge Wilson squinted down at his papers and read them slowly while the courtroom sat and waited with anticipation. Finally, the man raised his head and peered over at a well-dressed young attorney. "Mr. Morse, I see you are the prosecutor in this matter, but where is the counsel for the defense?"

"Mr. Clint Adams has refused counsel, Your Honor."

"That is not true!" Clint yelled, coming to his feet. "I never had a chance to see an attorney."

"Shut up!" Rankin said, driving an elbow into his ribs.

Clint gasped.

Judge Wilson ignored the blow. "Am I to interpret this to mean you, the defendant, wish to delay this trial until properly counseled?"

Clint raised his head, thought about the jail cell, and knew that he would not live to return to this courtroom. "No, Your Honor, I do not. I will speak in my own behalf."

"Very well," the judge said with approval. "Let the proceedings begin."

Mr. Morse fluttered out of his chair and moved to the center of the room. "This case," he began with a smile and a gesture to the packed courtroom, "clearly does not deserve the kind of attention it is receiving from our citizens. It is simply a matter of the harassment and molestation of a God-fearing lady, one of impeccable reputation.''

"I see," the judge said, staring at Clint. "Do you, Mr. Adams, wish to enter a plea of guilty? It would please the court to save the taxpayers both time and money.''

"No, sir! I am innocent.''

The judge scowled. "I was afraid you were going to say that. This damned black robe I am forced to wear is exceedingly hot and uncomfortable, and I am not pleased. The legal brief before me indicates this seems to be a very open and shut case. The lady in question, Miss Jennifer Neal, has submitted a sworn statement to the effect that you accosted her most rudely and then spoke lewd, suggestive words. When she ran, you grabbed her by the arm with great violence, and that is when Sheriff Rankin and his deputies intercepted you.''

"I had no designs on Miss Neal!''

The prosecuting attorney interrupted. "Your Honor, I know how uncomfortable you must be. We all are. I believe that a moment's testimony by Miss Neal will prove beyond a doubt that the charges are warranted and merit a stiff prison sentence.''

"Call the witness to the stand," Judge Wilson ordered grimly.

Clint straightened a little in his seat. He could sense the audience leaning forward with expectation because they wanted to know what lewdness he had whispered. When Miss Neal whisked by him, he smelled her perfume and saw again that remarkable figure of young womanhood that had already caused him such anguish.

God, he thought, staring at the beauty, she is almost worth the trouble I'm in now.

Her expression was composed, but it was clear she

was under considerable strain. Clint heard Rankin swallow noisily as the young woman was sworn in by the bailiff.

"Miss Neal," the judge began, "this is all very unfortunate, but it is a sign of these times when society's most lovely and decent flowers of womanhood are trampled upon by depraved men with bestial designs."

"I object," Clint yelled, springing to his feet.

"Silence him!"

The sheriff drove his elbow into Clint's face and dazed him for a moment. Satisfied, the judge said, "Now, Miss Neal, will you take a seat and then tell us exactly what the accused did and said to you?"

She nodded, clasped her hands in her lap, and said, "I was leaving John's . . . I mean Sheriff Rankin's office and was on my way back to my millinery shop when this . . . this total stranger came up to me and immediately said something like 'How do you feel after last night'?"

Women in the audience gasped and began to whisper, and the men grinned and leaned forward, transfixed.

"Silence in the courtroom!" the judge yelled, banging his gavel.

"Go on, Miss Neal," the prosecuting attorney urged, "tell the judge your immediate reaction."

"Shock. Simple shock. My first impression was that the man had mistaken me for someone else—or was drunk."

"And then your second impression was?"

She swallowed. "He seemed very excited. He acted as if we had been together and . . . I just sort of panicked, I guess, and began to run."

"And did he desist from his lecherous intentions?"

"Objection!" Clint shouted. "My intentions were not lecherous but . . ." His words died as Sheriff

Rankin reared back to punch him again. "Do that once more and you will eat these manacles," Clint said.

The judge pointed a finger at Clint, and he was shaking with fury. "Interrupt this court once more and I will have you gagged! You shall have your chance to speak."

The prosecuting attorney grinned at Clint because attorneys always detest men arrogant enough to try to represent themselves in a court of law.

"Go on, Miss Neal," the judge urged. "Tell me what followed."

Clint locked his teeth in a fury. The judge was supposed to be impartial. He had already made it abundantly clear he was not.

The young woman glanced at Clint or the sheriff and then whispered, "He said that we were going to make love under the stars. That was when he grabbed me."

The courtroom burst out in an uproar, and the judge had to pound his gavel over and over to restore order. When it was finally achieved, he said in a harsh voice, "One more outburst from this audience and I will have it removed!"

The only sound that followed was the droning of flies and the furious scratching of the court reporter's pen across paper.

The prosecuting attorney looked up to the judge as if he were a wounded animal and said in a beseeching voice, "Your Honor, my client has nothing else to say. The strain on her has been almost more than she can bear. I ask that she be excused."

Clint was on his feet in an instant. "Not yet, Your Honor. I demand to cross-examine Miss Neal."

"You sonofabitch!" Rankin hissed. "You are a dead man no matter what happens."

"Then I have nothing to lose," Clint growled, moving forward until he stood before the beautiful woman.

"Miss Neal, Honorable Judge Wilson, citizens of Tucson, forgive me my deplorable condition. I was not allowed to bathe or shave or even to wear a clean set of clothes to this courtroom. You cannot imagine how that makes me feel, but I can imagine the grief that I have caused . . . without any intention . . . to Miss Neal."

He steadied himself against the witness stand. "I promise you that I will not in any way compromise this beautiful and respectable young lady's honor during the next few minutes, but I must ask your indulgence. First, Miss Neal, did I show any additional personal concern for your welfare beyond asking how you were feeling? Did I not also ask if you were in any trouble?"

Their eyes locked and Clint saw that hers were red and that there was powder under them to hide dark circles. That encouraged him to think that this woman was not only lovely, but sensitive and troubled by this entire affair. She might well be drawn to his side of the argument if he handled his questions skillfully.

"Yes," she said after what seemed like an eternity. "You did."

"Thank you." He smiled broadly. "Miss Neal, are you by chance in any personal difficulty, perhaps with your fiancé, Sheriff Rankin?"

Clint heard the man curse and then heard the rapid scraping of boots as men sought to control the sheriff from attacking him. Clint ignored the threat and watched Miss Neal's expression. It told him what he had suspected all along—she was more afraid of Rankin than she had ever been of the Gunsmith. Rankin was forcing her to go through with this.

"No," she lied in a quavering voice.

Clint looked down at the floor and swallowed his disappointment. There was no chance that this poor, beautiful young lady was going to admit her fears.

"Miss Neal, you told the court that I was a total stranger. Isn't it true that our eyes met for a moment through the front window of O'Ginty's Saloon. Met just for a very, very special moment?"

She bit her lip. She nodded stiffly. "That is true, sir."

"So I was not, therefore, a total stranger."

"You acted so familiar! I felt as if . . ."

"What? Please, don't stop," Clint begged. "My very life may depend upon your candor."

"I felt as if you knew me in the . . . the carnal sense of the word, Mr. Adams."

The courtroom erupted in chaos and it took five minutes to quell the voices.

"I thought I did, Miss Neal. But I was wrong. You see, Mr. Sean O'Ginty saw our eyes meet, and he suggested he could arrange a rendezvous between us. He failed to tell me that you were an honorable woman, one engaged to be married to Sheriff Rankin. I was asleep in my own hotel room when an imposter came to me in the night and we . . . well, you know. That is why I mistook you for an intimate friend."

"But how could you do something like that to a woman and not know who . . . you must have at least heard her voice!"

Focusing on the girl, he felt that suddenly the entire courtroom vanished. It was as if they were alone together, just the two of them making up from some silly lover's quarrel. She seemed to lean toward him and to feel the same intimate intensity. "I did hear her and she stuttered so horribly that we talked scarcely at all. You see, Mr. O'Ginty tricked me because he wanted a portrait and I refused to remain in Tucson unless I had the chance to make your acquaintance. That is all I wanted, just to meet one as beautiful as yourself, perhaps even share dinner. That was all I asked, Miss Neal. All I dared to expect.''

Her eyes went misty and she dabbed at them with a silk scarf. ''Mr. Adams, I will not go through with—''

''Your Honor!'' shouted the prosecuting attorney, ''this is all very touching, but the defendant's words are without any foundation whatsoever! He must prove this . . . this wild fabrication we are hearing.''

''I can prove it, Your Honor. I call Mr. Sean O'Ginty to the witness stand.''

The judge frowned thoughtfully and everyone held his breath. ''Request approved. Summon Mr. O'Ginty to the witness stand.''

''Aw shit!'' Rankin wailed, ''Judge, what the hell—''

''Silence! I have given you and your deputies an order and I will not be questioned. Bring Mr. O'Ginty at once!''

Rankin's face flushed, and he whirled on his heel and stomped out of the courthouse.

Clint stood holding himself up weakly against the stand and gazing into the lovely eyes of Miss Neal. She was an angel and she believed him, but it had gone so far now that she would never be allowed to rescind her charges because the sheriff would not allow it.

He lost track of time. Suddenly, a voice shattered the hot silence when the sheriff burst back inside and yelled, ''O'Ginty has been murdered. Shot through the heart!''

Clint felt his knees buckle, and his world seemed to crash down on his shoulders. O'Ginty had been the only man who could have gotten him off free, and now he was dead.

After that, the case was open and shut. Within ten minutes the judge banged his gavel and intoned, ''I sentence you to two years in the state penitentiary at Yuma, sentence to be passed while engaged in hard labor! Court dismissed.''

Clint was yanked out of his seat and shoved toward the door. His eyes locked on those of Miss Jenny Neal as he passed, and he saw an abject misery in them.

All hope was gone.

ELEVEN

Clint was shoved into his cell, and when he bounced off the wall, the sheriff came at him like a blood-crazed animal. With his hands manacled together, Clint knew that he could not hope to defend himself, but he was ready to fight. Perhaps that was why he caught Rankin in the crotch with the toe of his boot and dropped him howling on the floor. Then, before the man could recover, Clint looped his wrists over Rankin's head and began to crush the man's throat with his manacles and chain.

The deputies drew their guns, and Clint knew that he was a dead man. There was no place to hide and no way to reach the sheriff's gun.

"Hold it!" Oscar Marsh shouted as he crashed through the doorway with Jenny Neal. "Don't you dare shoot that prisoner! Gunsmith, release the sheriff this instant!"

Clint was only too happy to obey that order and call a truce to this madness. The thought of spending two years in the penitentiary filled him with bitterness, but he would prefer that to being riddled to death.

"What is going on here?" Jenny Neal cried, kneeling beside the man she was engaged to marry. "Are you a depraved killer, Mr. Adams?"

Clint leaned up against a stone wall and tried to catch his breath. "No, ma'am, but I won't allow any man to beat me to death the way he was going to."

She paled, when she spoke again, her voice quavered slightly. "Is that true, John?"

Only now was the sheriff beginning to get his voice back. "I'll kill him yet!" he wheezed. "Kill him!"

"I heard that," Oscar Marsh shouted, "and if the Gunsmith is murdered while under your protection, I will demand there be a full investigation and that you go on trial for murder."

Rankin was shaking with rage, and apparently afraid he might go berserk and actually shoot Clint, Jenny Neal stepped between them. "John, please, don't be a murderer. Let this man go to prison without harm. The law has spoken. It is your duty to see that it is carried out."

"With pleasure!" the man breathed.

"Ask him to give you his word that he won't murder me in this cell," Clint demanded.

"John?"

"All right! He has my word."

Clint nodded. He staggered over to his thin mattress and collapsed. Strange as it sounded, he could hardly wait to get out of this death cage and be on his way to the penitentiary. At least there he was sure he had a chance of coming out alive. But not much of a chance.

He had visited the penitentiary at Yuma a number of times. Once, a friend of his named Charley Taylor had been sentenced to eighteen months hard labor for killing a man who had intended to kill him first.

Clint remembered that he had hardly recognized Charley after he had been at Yuma six months; Charley had aged twenty years. His face was scorched brown by the sun and wind, his body was as twisted as the gnarled bough of a dead pine tree. Charley had suffered from heat stroke the second July he had endured the chain gang. His heart had stopped pumping, and when they put him in the rocky ground, they said the pine box and his body together did not weigh one hundred pounds—the day he walked into the penitentiary, Charlie weighed better than two hundred pounds. They had broken the man down to a skeleton.

Yuma was hell. The prisoners were kept in dirt caves that afforded some relief from the punishing desert heat. But you worked hard at Yuma on the rock piles and chain gangs, and few men lived through two summers. And for an ex-lawman, the chances of surviving were far worse.

Clint swallowed, knowing that once inside the prison he was a dead man.

Oscar Marsh came to visit him on Tuesday, and he sneaked in a small ham and some hard-boiled eggs that Clint ate with a raging hunger.

"How did you get them to let you in here?" he asked when he finished eating.

"I paid the sheriff fifty dollars."

"That's all?" Given Rankin's personal hatred of him, Clint was surprised the man agreed to this concession for so little money.

"That's equal to his monthly salary," Oscar said.

"What do you want from me?"

Oscar reached inside his coat and pulled out a contract. "Sign it and I will do all I can to get an immediate retrial."

"You wouldn't have a chance."

"What chance do you have now?"

"None," Clint said tightly. "Leave the damned contract here and I'll look it over later."

Oscar grinned. "Knew you'd come around to seeing it my way. I can show you the best time of your life, Gunsmith. Make everything all right again—make you an overnight sensation."

"Just like a magic fairy, huh?"

"I don't care for that comparison, but use it if it amuses."

Clint asked, "How can you make everything right for me here in Arizona?"

"Cigar?"

Clint rarely smoked, but these were better than cheroots, and so he nodded yes. Then he let Oscar light them up. The fine tobacco was mild, yet rich and relaxing.

"I can only say this, Gunsmith. Money talks. I found that out a long, long time ago. Some people are easily corruptible, some resist mightily for a while, but everyone has his price. The sheriff's was only fifty dollars. Judge Wilson's might be ten times that, but it is still a question of dollars. All that is required is to find the price and pay."

"Jesus," Clint said with a scowl, "I would hate to think that your way of reasoning is true. I've met men who would never sell out for any price."

"Perhaps you never dug deep enough to find the right price. For example, I offered you, what—a hundred dollars a week?"

"Guaranteed."

"And you turned it down in so abruptly that I immediately sensed that you would not accept the offer even had I doubled or tripled it. True?"

"Yes."

"So," Oscar said, puffing great clouds of smoke, "I said to myself, Oscar, this man's price is not money. Perhaps it is women. After all, a woman got you into this predicament. O'Ginty knew right away that your price was a woman seen through a window."

"But never again."

"All right," Oscar agreed, "I anticipated that, and

after thinking it out very carefully, I knew that a man such as yourself could not be bought or sold. Your pride is not your weakness, for you obviously cared nothing about starring in my show. So, I had to ask myself what was your price? What would a man such as yourself prize above all? Prize so highly he would sign the dotted line of a five-year contract?''

Clint inhaled deeply and stared at the man before him. He had to admit that Oscar Marsh was one of the smartest hucksters he had ever met and easily the best judge of character.

"It's pretty obvious what you came up with," Clint said, his words showing no anger. "You sized me up and told yourself that what I valued most of all was my freedom and my reputation as a decent, honest man despite all the blood I have spilled in the line of duty."

"Exactly so!" Oscar grinned. "I didn't know whether freedom or reputation was the more important to you, but it didn't matter. I did know that you would sign my contract if either were taken away."

"It almost sounds as if—"

"God himself intended to help me? Yes, I know," Oscar admitted. "Suddenly, you lost both and you are without a friend in this town except myself. I have always been lucky, Gunsmith. I call this luck."

Clint gazed at the paper beside him. "If I sign and go to prison, the contract is void?"

"Of course!"

"I am due to leave for Yuma under guard early in the morning."

Oscar Marsh pulled out his gold watch. "It is six o'clock and I have a dinner engagement with Judge Wilson at seven. Let's see, I sense a highly developed greediness in him, so we should cut through the trivialities by seven and reach his price by eight o'clock this evening. Then, a cigar and a brandy or two to settle the deal. I think this could all be over for you by ten o'clock at the very latest. By ten-thirty, you will be doing whatever you choose."

"Taking a bath, putting on clean clothes, having a nice dinner and a bottle of whiskey, hugging my horse, then riding—"

"No. Riding nowhere, Gunsmith. That contract states that your employment begins immediately. The citizens of this town must be appeased, so the judge will order a quick retrial and a stuttering woman will be produced to corroborate your story. Then, I propose we leave for Yuma. Just think, instead of being a prisoner on his way to hell, you will be dressed well and be tutored by myself as we begin to prepare an act based on your illustrious career as a lawman."

"To play in Yuma in the summer?"

"Hmmm, perhaps you are right. Very well then, we will go on to San Diego and book their finest hall. That will be your stage debut. We need to perfect our show in the west and find a couple of stock actors to play outlaws before we conquer the eastern seaboard. So, after San Diego, we will tour Los Angeles, then Virginia City, and finally San Francisco. That is a town!"

"Does sound better than the Yuma pen," Clint said without enthusiasm. "I suppose it is stupid to ask, but will there be any truth whatsoever in what I am supposed to tell the masses?"

Oscar Marsh almost looked grieved at the question. "There is always a grain of truth in everything my stars say. In the case of Jake Bosco, I admit that we stretched the truth pretty far—in your case, we might only have to embellish the truth somewhat."

"And I would still have to do gun tricks and fake fights?" The thought of acting out the killing of men was something Clint knew he would have trouble with; he just carried too many memories of the real thing inside.

"Of course. That is what the people want to see—the Gunsmith in action! It will be wonderful not having to teach someone how to draw and fire rapidly. But you will have to slow down every other night."

"Why?"

"So that an outlaw can kill you!" Oscar Marsh stood up, his eyes alive with excitement. "I shall give you or your victim—whichever of you is supposed to be gunned down in the street that evening—a vial of catsup. When you are hit, you slap your chest where the bullets are supposed to enter your body and scream, "My God, I am shot! I am dead!"

Clint groaned, already mortified by the image of himself up on a stage shouting those words.

"Then," Marsh said, jabbing the cigar at him, "you groan very loudly, shriek once or twice, and do a complete spin on your toes as if the bullets are lifting you up in your agony. You crash to the floor. Isn't that wonderful? The crowds always love it!"

Clint picked up the contract and read it over quickly, even as his mind was remembering Charley Taylor and what they had done to him at Yuma. "Give me your pen," he said.

"You won't regret this. Smartest thing you have ever done in your life."

Clint quickly scribbled his signature on the contract. "Go buy the judge," he said.

"Yes! Yes, of course! But you understand that whatever I must pay him is deducted from your salary."

Clint grabbed the contract from the man. "I don't remember reading that."

"You didn't," Oscar said. "But that is the way it will be—take it or leave it."

The man was probably bluffing, but Clint was in no position to find out. He shoved the contract in Oscar Marsh's face and watched the man bolt for the door.

TWELVE

Clint kept staring at the clock on the wall above the sheriff's desk all evening long. At six o'clock he envisioned Oscar Marsh and the judge meeting, shaking hands, and then sharing a drink before dinner. Then the meal itself and still they were making small talk. At eight, Clint imagined the two men starting to get right down to the serious business of money and a retrial with full dismissal of the charges. When nine o'clock came around, Clint felt sure that the deal had been set.

It was a quarter to ten and Clint's nerves were raw with anticipation when he heard a woman's voice whisper through the bars of the cell window.

"Mr. Adams!"

Clint stiffened. There was a deputy not twenty feet away who kept glancing toward his cell every five or ten minutes as if he were also expecting something important to happen.

"Mr. Adams!" The woman's voice was louder, more insistent this time.

Clint stood up and leaned against the wall, placing his head beside the window. "I'm listening," he whispered.

"It's Jenny Neal. I have to warn you that John is—"

He heard her sob. "Is what?" Clint asked.

"Is out of control and drinking heavily at the saloon. I'm afraid for your life. I don't know what to do!"

"Neither do I," he whispered. "Not unless you find me a gun very quickly."

"I can't do that!"

Clint said, "Thanks anyway. Go home, Jenny."

He heard footsteps receding down the alley. Clint drew in a deep breath. Now, it was just a matter of who got to him first—the sheriff or Oscar Marsh.

The next few minutes seemed to last forever. Finally, he heard footsteps on the boardwalk and he stood up to grip the bars. "Let it be Oscar Marsh!" he whispered.

The door swung open and there stood the young sheriff, his eyes wild and bloodshot. "Phil, get the hell out of here for a while. I'll take over."

The deputy looked from his boss to Clint and then smiled tightly. "Sure, John. And if I see Ed or the others, I'll tell them to stay away until I hear that you have taken care of our friend."

Clint cursed in helpless fury as the sheriff approached. His gait was unsteady, and there was a wild, half-crazed look in his eyes.

"So, Gunsmith, your fat eastern partner is going to try to buy your freedom, is that the way of things?"

Buy time, Clint told himself, trying to steady his nerves. "I don't know what you mean."

"The hell you don't! Judge Wilson and that Marsh fella are laughing and telling jokes, having themselves a real party over at the Ranch House Restaurant. Steak, champagne, they might as well advertise the deal in the newspaper! The judge sold me out. He is going to regret that. I promise he will."

"Listen, why don't we talk this over and see if we can make a deal. You want money? Oscar Marsh will pay you to keep me alive."

"You beggin'?" the arrogant young lawman asked with a sneer.

Clint rocked back on his heels. "Hell, no! I just decided Oscar Marsh was right and that we all have a price. I thought you might as well profit the same as the judge. Make some money. Buy Miss Neal a fine house, clothes, and things. You'd like that, wouldn't you?''

"I'd buy myself a better horse and saddle. I need a new rifle, too. Keep the rest for the whiskey and ladies. You understand. A man was never meant to drink from the same cup of honey every day."

Clint thought he saw a shadow move behind the sheriff. Oscar Marsh? Another deputy?

"I tell you this, Gunsmith. Before I kill you, I have to say my only regret is that I'll never have the chance to prove I am faster than you."

"I regret it, too. Give me a gun and let's find out."

John Rankin giggled. "You'd like that, wouldn't you? Take me on when I been drinking hard. Uh-uh. I ain't that drunk."

He went over and got the keys to the cell. "Stand back while I unlock the cell. Stand back I say or I'll drill you right now and drag your body out!"

Clint stepped back. He was desperate to look to the doorway, but afraid that if he did, the sheriff might catch the movement of his eyes and spin around and fire his gun.

The key clicked into the keyhole. "That's far enough, Gunsmith. You got any prayers, say 'em now because I'm sending you to the promised land."

"John, no!"

Jenny Neal stood in the doorway with a gun shaking in her fist, one Clint was sure she had intended somehow to pass through the cell bars to him. "John, I can't let you murder someone."

The sheriff smiled lopsidedly and began to move toward her. "Jenny, Jenny darlin', you pretend you never seen or heard anything and let me—"

"Drop your gun, John! Drop it, I say!"

The sheriff's voice grew cold and threatening. "Jenny, we're going to be married and I won't have my woman interfering in my business."

"Is your business murder?"

Clint reached through the bars and frantically worked at the key. Two seconds later, the lock snapped and the door swung open.

"Give me that gun, Jenny!"

Clint lunged for the sheriff's gun hand as the man reached for Jenny. Clint heard the roar of gunfire, and then the lawman was spinning around with a bullet wound in his side. Clint ripped the gun from the sheriff's hand, and when the man started to climb to his feet, he pistol-whipped Rankin across the forehead and vaulted for the doorway.

"Thanks!" he whispered gratefully. "I'd be dead by now if it had not been for you."

"He might even have killed me, too," she whispered. "He'll get well and make me pay dearly."

"In that case," Clint said, "I suggest you and I both find a good place to hide until we can figure a way out of this mess. Come on!"

Jenny Neal stared down at the sheriff, and then she grabbed up her skirts. Together, they raced out of the office and dodged into the first side alley they could find.

Clint smashed over a trash barrel and a stray cat hissed and screamed as he accidentally stepped on its tail.

"Where are we going?"

"Damned if I know," Clint gasped as he pulled her along through the blackness.

They burst onto a residential side street, and Clint froze as horses' hooves thundered their approach in the night. Clint threw his arm across Jenny's shoulders and suddenly he was acting like a stumbling drunk as three men raced their horses toward them. Jenny Neal needed no explanations. She was wearing a hat, and now she giggled uproariously and swayed, too, the picture of a drunken whore with money to be made if her cowboy friend did not pass out first.

The riders slowed for only a moment and then galloped on past. Clint pulled his arm free and they hurried forward. "I hope you have a place in mind to hide," he grunted, "because I am lost."

They rushed on for a block before she said, "I know a place where they will never find us."

"Is it far?"

"No, not very far at all."

They heard shouts, angry but indistinguishable. Clint did not have to guess that a posse was being formed. The stables and all the horses would quickly be covered to avoid any chance of escape, and then the town would be searched street by street. The sheriff would tell everyone that the Gunsmith had shot him and then kidnapped Jenny Neal. The people of Tucson would hunt them relentlessly. No one would give them sanctuary.

But Clint wasn't complaining. Maybe it would have been better if Oscar Marsh had arrived to announce his deal and spring him from the jail on bond. But that was conjecture and this was real. Beside him was the most beautiful creature he had seen in years, and she was terrified of the man she was supposed to marry. That gave Clint a little extra motivation to get his name cleared and bring Sheriff Rankin and his men to justice.

They were a nest of vipers, and for everyone's sake they needed to be eliminated.

THIRTEEN

They ducked through a couple of yards and then down a dry river bed at what Clint guessed was the southern end of town. All along the river bed were big cottonwood and sycamore trees. That told Clint that an underground river flowed here and that the river probably filled up after a heavy desert cloudburst. When they had gone about a half mile beyond the nearest house, Jenny stopped.

Clint tried to sound hopeful, but it wasn't easy. "Jenny, they'll come looking for us here first light. They'll ride a circle around the town, and these trees will be where they'd expect a fugitive to hide."

"When I was a girl, we lived not far away from here. In the spring, there are pools after the hard water rushes by, and sometimes they stay filled for months. Me and my brothers used to swim in them. We had a fine house, Clint. My father was a well-to-do man, a builder and an architect."

"I'm glad you had a nice childhood, but . . ."

"We loved to hike and play out here, and so we built the most wonderful tree house in the world—one so high and so fine that it was safe and secret from anyone. My brothers grew up to be like my father. They were very talented with a hammer, saw, and nails."

"That's where we are going? To a tree house?"

"Yes, and we are standing right under it."

Clint craned his neck and looked up into the great canopy of dark limbs and leaves. He could not see a thing. The tree's trunk was gigantic. The tree must have been a hundred feet high. "How do we get up there?"

"I'll show you."

Jenny moved to a low, flat rock, and Clint had to help her move it aside to reveal a rope and a grappling hook and a bottle of soda pop.

"How long has this stuff been here?" he asked, testing the rope in his hands and satisfying himself that it was not rotted through.

"Since my last brother got married and moved to Los Angeles three years ago. The soda pop was our treat for making the climb. I hope it is still good."

Clint slipped the bottle under his belt. "No reason it shouldn't be."

"You need to throw the hook up to the first branch and then climb the rope. Once there, you can step and climb from limb to limb. But we never did it at night."

Clint expelled a deep breath. He was not in his usual good condition or up to strength, but there seemed little choice but to try the climb. "Stand back, Jenny. This hook looks pretty mean."

He tried throwing it a half dozen times without success, which did not surprise him because above was total darkness. Jenny tried when his arm gave out, and she seemed to know exactly where and how hard to throw the hook. On the second toss, it caught.

"I'll be damned," Clint said. "How do you know it caught the right branch?"

"I just do. Here, you follow me."

She lifted up her skirts and he wished he could have seen the shape of her leg, but he could not. He boosted her up the rope and then she vanished.

"Come on up," she called down to him. "You will need me to show the way."

"That is for damned sure," he grunted, gripping the hemp rope in his fists and locking it between his thighs as he started up into the darkness.

By the time his head bumped into a stout limb, Clint's arm muscles were on fire. He grabbed the limb and pulled himself up onto it, and the sensation of being about twenty feet up in total darkness was not one that he relished one bit. But at her urging, he took hold of her skirt. They began the very slow and careful climb from branch to branch. It seemed to take hours, but finally Jenny took his hand in her own and lifted it until they touched the smoothed side of a sawed piece of timber.

"We are touching our door," she told him.

"It is incredible," Clint whispered, following her up onto a flat surface. They crawled forward and bumped into something that scooted across the board floor.

"What's that?"

"A bed. There is also a table and two chairs."

He stood up cautiously, for he did not know high the ceiling was. He discovered it was only about five feet—ample room for a kid but not an adult.

"Isn't it a wonderful tree house? It once had glass windows, but in storms the tree limbs would whip around and break them."

"It is a miracle of workmanship. How did you get all this up here?"

"We dropped a long rope and pulled it up. My brothers were very inventive. We had great fun here. I always felt . . ."

"What?"

"Safe here. I love to lie on the floor and listen to the leaves singing in the breeze at night. It seems cooler here, too."

Clint felt his way around, but suddenly a section of the flooring gave away under his weight and he dropped and would have gone through had he not instinctively thrown out his arms.

"Help, Jenny, help me, but be careful!" he said, trying to pull himself up before more of the flooring broke away.

She understood, and completely disregarding her own safety, she threw herself across the floor and grabbed his arms.

Clint's legs were dangling; he had to fight like crazy to pull himself up, for the broken boards seemed to lock him in place. But with Jenny's help he pulled up and back onto solid flooring. Then they rolled away and lay panting from the exertion.

"Are you all right?"

The boards had scratched his chest and back pretty bad. "I'll live," he groaned.

"You are hurt, aren't you?"

Before he could answer, she was pulling up his shirt, feeling along his ribs and touching the blood. It made her begin to cry and she hugged his neck.

"Hey," he said, pulling her close, "I'll live. I'm just scratched up. It's all right."

"No, it's not," she whispered. "This is all my fault. If I hadn't panicked when you mistook me for another woman, none of this would have happened!"

"It is not your fault, Jenny. None of it. I wanted to meet you. That's what started the trouble. I thought I might even be lucky enough to steal a kiss in the moonlight."

"There is no moonlight in the middle of a tree," she sniffled.

"I don't need it, do you?"

When her lips searched out and found his own, Clint

guessed she did not. Perhaps it was because they were in such desperate straits, or even that they prevailed over John Rankin this night, but for whatever reason, Clint found himself wanting very much to make love to this woman.

Jenny seemed to feel the same need and physical hunger. She was pulling up her skirts and helping him yank down her underclothing. Clint could hear her breath coming loud and fast as he bent over her and undid the buttons that constricted her breasts.

She moaned and pressed his face down into her sweet, soft flesh, and he found one, then the other of her rigid nipples.

"Oh, Gunsmith," she moaned, "I have to say I wanted you like this from the moment I saw you through the saloon window."

To prove her words, she reached down and quickly found his rigid manhood. Her hips arched up and Clint slammed his hips forward to drive himself deep into her.

"Oooh," she groaned with a shudder that made her heels drum on the tree house floor. "I have never made love to a gunfighter and never in a tree house before."

Clint panted, "Me neither, beautiful lady. I got a hunch this is going to be quite a night for the both of us."

Jenny nipped at his ear, probed it with her wet tongue, grabbed his buttocks hard, and began to rotate.

Clint nipped at her breasts until she was crying out with pleasure. The Yuma penitentiary and Oscar Marsh with his hated contract seemed like things from another world as he stroked into the woman deep and strong, seeking nothing but to lose himself in her completely. Tomorrow, they would stay hidden here until the search exhausted itself or moved farther out. After that, they would have to leave this place, but until then . . .

"Oh Gunsmith! I'm coming, I'm . . . ohhh, yes!"

The tree house rocked and the leaves danced around them. Clint covered her mouth with his own so that her screams could not be heard all the way to Tucson. And when she hit her highest note, he grabbed her buttocks and filled her until they both lay drained and locked in a lover's embrace.

FOURTEEN

They slept well past daybreak. Clint was awakened by the sound of voices and horseshoes clipping rock. He rolled to his haunches and scrubbed sleep from his eyes before peering around and assuring himself that, yes, this was really happening and he was out of jail and perched high up in a massive sycamore tree with a beautiful woman at his side.

When Jenny Neal stirred, he reached and gently cupped his hand over her mouth just in case she might awaken with a startled cry. He need not have worried. Her eyes opened and he felt her lips smile under his hand.

"Good morning," he said in a hushed voice. "We are about to have visitors pass under us."

"Oh, not yet!" she whispered with sudden alarm.

"What's wrong? They'll never see us up here."

"I know that, but we forgot to pull up the rope. It was dark and it was all we could do to make it up here. I decided to risk waiting until daylight. If they see it, we are trapped!"

Clint was already moving. He eased to the door and grabbed a branch and then dangled for a moment before his feet located another step. Next, he was descending just as quickly as was humanly possible.

The voices and the sounds of the horses were coming very near. Clint knew full well that a dangling rope would catch their attention and demand further investigation.

He could see them now: five heavily armed riders searching for tracks, for any sign two people fleeing in the night might leave—an overturned rock revealing dark, damp soil underneath; a thread or scrap of Jenny's skirt torn by brush; a clear footprint.

Clint was almost to the grappling hook now, two more branches and . . . he lost his footing. The bark seemed to twist out from under his boot and he stifled a shout as he dropped four feet and then wildly threw his arms out. He just managed to grab another branch. The fall was almost enough to pop his arms out of their sockets, and for a moment, it was all he could do to hang on.

Feet waving, searching for a limb to straddle, he reached out and snagged the grappling hook.

His face was pressed against the bark, which was covered with wood ants. They began to crawl across his cheeks as he worked to pull the rope up into the veil of limbs and branches. An ant stung him on an eyelid and it felt like a nettle. It burned fiercely, but he paid it no attention as he pulled the rope up.

A moment later, the riders passed almost directly underneath. Clint hung there motionless, not even daring to breathe until they were far up the dry river bed. Then he reached up and slapped the ants from his face before slowly climbing back up to the tree house and rolling onto its floor where he lay gasping.

"I'm sorry," Jenny said. "I should have remembered. Here, have some soda pop."

Clint popped the cork and drank, finding the sweet drink was still delicious. He thanked her and crawled onto the bed and collapsed from his sudden and strenuous exertions.

He must have dozed off because when he awoke it

was high noon and the sun was filtering down through the branches. The air was still and hot as an oven. But as hot as it was, Clint knew it was still ten to fifteen degrees cooler than out on the desert floor.

"Are you feeling better?" Jenny asked, looking down at this whiskered, ant-bitten face.

Clint kissed her and then he pulled her up and onto him. Jenny hugged him fiercely and then they made love again, slower this time, slow and easy, knowing that they had all day and that there was no guarantee about tomorrow.

Later, Clint asked, "How come a beautiful woman like yourself wants to marry such a man as John Rankin?"

She shrugged. "John was my former husband's best friend. He is not the man he was even six months ago when he was just a deputy."

"Who was your first husband?"

"He was the town's former sheriff. John was his best deputy. They became very close friends."

"Did your husband die in the line of duty?"

"Yes. He tried to stop a bank robbery four months ago. It was on a Tuesday morning and six men just rode into town and hit the bank. The manager tried to resist and they gunned him down. My husband was on duty. He grabbed his rifle and raced out into the street, and two of the bank robbers stationed beside the door killed him. The doctor said that he died instantly."

"Rankin and the other deputies—where were they at the time?"

"John and the only other deputy at that time had ridden out before dawn to investigate the murder of a prospector. By the time they returned to Tucson, the bank robbers were far away. John and Phil said they tracked them for three days, but the trail went cold in New Mexico, and they had to come back empty-handed."

"And Rankin inherited your husband's office and wife."

Jenny smiled sadly. "He was very, very kind to me at first. I needed someone to talk to because my brothers were all gone and my parents both dead. I leaned on John for support and he was strong—a perfect gentleman until one night when he knocked on my door." Jenny took a deep breath. "I had been in bed asleep, and when I called out to ask who it was, he gave me his name and said he was hurt."

"Was he?"

"Sort of. He had been in some kind of terrible saloon brawl and had been cut with a knife, but not badly. His face was bruised and one eye swollen almost shut. I couldn't turn him away, but when he came inside, I realized that he was drunk and that he wanted to do it to me."

"You asked him to leave?"

"Yes! I threatened to yell. He laughed and asked me who was going to come, that he was the sheriff and that he was in the middle of an investigation."

She took in a deep breath. "He investigated me, Gunsmith. All of me. I fought him but that only seemed to excite him even more. I don't know how many times he raped me that night, four, perhaps five."

A tear rolled down her cheek and Clint brushed it away. "You don't have to say more, Jenny."

"I want to. The next morning I was expecting some lady friends for tea and cookies. I foolishly told John, and when they knocked on the door, he called them in making sure that my bedroom door was open."

Jenny groaned. "When those respectable ladies

walked in—oh, I was so ashamed because there we were in bed and John was doing it to me and—I heard a platter of cookies crash on the floor and—"

"Stop," Clint said, covering her lips with his own. "Don't say another word, or ever think about it again."

She nodded. "I'll try not to. But you can see how it was then. I knew that I either had to marry the man or leave Tucson branded a whore. There is not much in between for a woman who has been publicly compromised. John understood that just as well. I have a millinery shop and it is profitable, but if my reputation were destroyed, then I might as well have given the business away."

"You could open a shop somewhere else," Clint suggested.

"I love Tucson. I love this tree house and this country is where I belong. Something in me refused to be driven away from a business that took me five years to build and friends that I have known all my life. I have roots here. Until I find a man I love and will marry, then here I shall stay."

She studied his battered, bewhiskered face. "But if that man asked me to go with him somewhere far away, for whatever reason, then I would follow him to the ends of the earth. I want you to remember that, Gunsmith."

The implication was clear. "I'm not that man, Jenny, but you'll find him one of these days and he will make you happy if he has any intelligence at all. Anyway, my name is Clint, not the Gunsmith. I think we are well enough acquainted to call each other by our first names, don't you?"

She laughed. "I should hope so! Clint?"

"Yes?"

"We have to have food and water by tonight. What are we going to do?"

"We go back into Tucson and we get them. I must find that stuttering woman and get her to see the judge. If Wilson won't alter his verdict and drop all charges against me, then I will find another way to clear my name."

"If O'Ginty were still alive, he could settle everything."

"Yeah," Clint said with a frown. "But he isn't and I intend to bring his killer to justice."

"Do you think it was John?"

"He is certainly at the top of my list of suspects," Clint said. "Now, why don't we each have a sip of that soda pop and try to rest through the heat of the day. Tonight is going to be very busy for us."

"Couldn't be busier than last night."

Clint grinned broadly. "No," he conceded, "I guess it couldn't."

FIFTEEN

It was in full darkness that they moved toward Jenny's small house, and the gun in Clint's hand was ready in case Rankin had thought to post a guard.

There was no guard, no reception committee, so they moved inside. While Jenny set plates of cold food on the table by candlelight, Clint took the opportunity to take a bath before he shaved with her deceased husband's razor and then dressed in his clothes. From a dresser drawer, he removed a well-oiled gun and holster. The cartridge belt was full, and when Clint tested the gun, he found it in perfect working order. He buckled it around his waist, and from the indentation in the leather, he could tell that Jenny's late husband had the same waist size. After slicking back his hair and trying on the man's hat, he studied himself in the mirror, and except for the hollowness of his cheeks and one swollen eyelid, he looked almost normal.

"What do you think?" he asked, stepping into the kitchen.

Her trembling smile told Clint that he looked a little too much like her late husband, so he just kissed Jenny on the cheek and they sat down and ate.

"I think it would be better if you stayed here until I returned," Clint said. "If the woman I seek is still in Tucson, then she will be found in the red-light district. It is not a place for you to go."

"I would rather come with you. What if John should come back or send someone here to check if we have returned?"

"All right," Clint said, "then come along."

Once on the street, they moved casually as if out for an evening's stroll or a visit. Clint admired the wide, clean streets and the neat little wooden houses with their carefully tended gardens surrounded by white picket fences to keep out kids and dogs.

"This is a part of town I have never seen," he admitted as they walked along.

"There is no reason you should have. It is the nicest part of town, and I know that sounds awful, but it is true. What you see belongs to the merchants and businessmen and a few comfortably retired people—the backbone of the community."

"I'd never fit in a neighborhood like this. It is too . . . respectable and proper."

"Bathed and dressed in nice clothes, you are entirely respectable. I would judge you to be, oh, a successful saddlemaker or gunsmith."

"I actually am a gunsmith, but I usually work out of a wagon. I like the freedom it gives me to go from town to town."

"Don't you ever think of having a permanent establishment?"

"Yeah," he admitted, "when I turn sixty, I am going to give that a lot of hard thought. Until then, however, I think I'll be content to follow my fancy wherever that might lead."

She shook her head. "Some day some woman will catch you. I just guess I am not the woman and this is not the time."

Clint let the subject lie there without further comment. He liked women, and he liked variety. There had been many that he had considered spending a lot of time with, but not permanently.

Now, as they entered the side of town where women

of the night plied their trade, he was reminded that he
had a particular woman to find—a beautiful stuttering
woman. She should not be overly difficult to find
because this section of town was dominated by only
three or four houses of prostitution.

Which one, he asked himself, could O'Ginty have
found her in? She had been a very extraordinary tigress
in bed. Someone was bound to know of her.

Easily the most impressive brothel was a two-story
Gothic building in perfect shape. A bouncer with a hard
face and a rough voice stopped them. "You here to
gawk or what?"

"I want to see the madam."

The bouncer peered at Jenny with a professional eye.
"What's she want, a job?"

Clint almost reached for the man, but Jenny's voice
stopped him cold. "That's right, honey. This is my man
and we need some money."

The bouncer struck a match with his thumbnail and
studied Jenny even closer. "I'll pay you five dollars
right now," he breathed, reaching out to touch her
breast.

Clint's gun was cocked and poking into the man's
face faster than the blink of an eye. The bouncer
dropped his match and reared back, his hands coming
up. "Don't shoot, man! I was just trying to help you
two out. Five dollars is more'n she'll get each time she
does it for Madam Lola."

"Why don't you let us talk to her and decide?"

"Sure! Whatever you say!"

The bouncer led them through the parlor, and as
Clint glanced down a narrow hallway, he saw a roomful
of men and painted ladies drinking and talking. It was,
he knew, the parlor, a place where the drinks were expensive and watered down.

Madam Lola's room was on the second floor at the head of the steps, and her door stayed open so that she could watch who came up and who went down. She was a big woman, dissipated and fortyish with massive sagging breasts and baggy pockets under both eyes. She had probably once been a leggy redhead and pretty; now, the years and the booze had left her face blotched and her mouth was a slash of bright red lipstick.

"What the hell is this? Visitors' hour?" she demanded in a shrill voice.

The bouncer shifted under her whipping voice. "She wants to talk to you about a job."

Lola's shrewd little eyes flicked over Jenny like the tip of a rapier. "She's not here for work. This is Sheriff Rankin's woman, you damn fool! Get back to your post!"

The man's face turned ugly and he whirled around and stomped down the steep flight of stairs.

"Now," the madam said, motioning them both forward, "tell me what the hell is really on your minds. You are the Gunsmith, and you are Miss Jenny Neal, widow of our late sheriff whom I liked one hell of a lot better than your current fiancé."

"How do you know so much?" Clint asked.

"How? Because it is my business to know what is going on in Tucson. I have a back door; all my competitors have the same. We entertain the so-called respectable citizens of this town, the politicians, the judge, others like them. I will tell you, Jenny, that your late husband was never here for pleasure and neither did he go to anyone else for flesh."

"Thank you," she said gratefully.

"But your young peacock, John Rankin, comes in the front door of this place and all the rest with great regularity. You should know that right now. The man is a degenerate. If he were not the sheriff, my girls would have nothing to do with him, and I wouldn't blame them a bit."

"I am looking for a woman," Clint said.

"I heard you never paid for it, Gunsmith."

"I don't. The woman I seek is also quite lovely. She is about the size and shape of Miss Neal."

"What's her name?"

"I don't know."

"Got a picture? A description?"

"No, nothing." Clint shifted, feeling slightly embarrassed. "I thought she was Miss Neal the night we made love. It was very dark. All I can tell you is that she, well, she stutters."

Madam Lola had started to laugh, but now her thick red lips pursed thoughtfully. She reached around behind her to light a thin black cigar. She lit it, sucked deeply, and exhaled, letting the smoke filter out of both nostrils dragonlike. "Now, I begin to understand it a little," she mused almost to herself.

Clint stepped forward. "Understand what? Lady, if you can shed some light on this, it would mean a whole hell of a lot to me."

"Sure it would. How much is it worth to you, Gunsmith?"

His shoulders slumped. "I don't have any money," he said. "You know that I have been in jail and sentenced to the Yuma pen."

"What about you, honey? You got some money, don't you?"

Jenny opened her handbag, dug out all the money she had, and offered it to the madam. "It is not much more than ten or fifteen dollars, but I can—"

"It'll do. Put it on the table over there and then both of you sit down for a minute while I think this over."

"Appreciate it if you'd think out loud," Clint told the madam.

"All right, here it is. Maybe you can fit the pieces. O'Ginty came racing in here about the time I heard you had arrived, Gunsmith. He said he had to have a woman."

"I told him fine, that he could have his pick starting with me!" Lola chuckled. "I liked the cut of that man, his big strong shoulders."

"Go on with the story," Clint said, trying to hide his annoyance.

"Well, I had a new girl then. Her name is Sherry and she is hot in bed. I mean she loves the work! And, though she is old for the trade—probably thirty and that is very old in this business—she is still pretty because she doesn't drink too hard and does exercises every morning and drinks a glass of milk before going to bed. Every night, a glass of milk."

Clint wished the madam would get along with her story, but he knew better than to risk annoying her and having her clam up completely.

"So I told O'Ginty about Sherry, and when he saw her, he said she was just the thing he needed. Next thing I know, Sherry is practicing a stutter!"

"She was!"

"Yep. It was the damnedest thing you ever saw, and all the girls thought it was just hysterical, but Sherry kept right on stuttering."

"She's the one," Clint said. "Where is she now?"

"She upped and quit."

Clint groaned. "Do you know where I can find her?"

"She left a message, or rather the man she ran away with left a message that I didn't understand at the time, but it was so strange that I still remember. The man said that if anyone famous should ask, tell him the contract remains valid and we will be in Phoenix.''

''I don't suppose this man was in his late fifties, fat, and with bunch of diamonds on his fingers.''

''That's the one! Kinda cute, too, when he shut up long enough to take a breath.''

''The Legend Maker,'' Clint said.

''Huh?''

''His name is Oscar Marsh and he is a promoter, a huckster, and about the shrewdest man I have ever run across. Thanks, Lola.''

She blew smoke across at them. ''You come back, Clint, honey, and I'll give it to you for free—all you want, whenever you want. O'Ginty had the right idea—you'd be good for business. Customers might just like the idea of screwin' the same girl the Gunsmith himself screwed.''

''No,'' Clint said with a violent shake of his head. ''But thanks anyway.''

They hurried down the stairs, and when the bouncer took a passing swing at Clint, he ducked and the man's fist smashed into the door. He howled in pain.

Clint hurried on, Jenny clinging to his arm.

He had no intention of brawling with the bouncer; there wasn't time. They were headed for Phoenix, and whether Oscar Marsh knew it yet or not, the contract he had signed was void. The fast-talking easterner had not delivered him from prison—Jenny had and that meant he was still a free man. At least he was until he either settled this mess or the law captured him.

SIXTEEN

Clint eased his gun out of his holster as he approached the dark livery stable where Duke was boarded. He had no idea if Sheriff Rankin had posted a guard or not, but it seemed likely that he had, given that much of his reputation was earned riding the big gelding. It was common knowledge that he greatly valued his horse.

He pulled Jenny Neal close and whispered in her ear, "You wait right here, and if there is no trouble, come on in after me."

She nodded and Clint edged up to the big livery with its huge wooden doors. He gripped one and found that it was not bolted from the inside, so he pulled it open a crack and peered into the darkness. He could see nothing. But he could hear the familiar stomping of horses and their soft sounds of welcome.

Clint slipped inside, gun up and ready. He moved slowly, trying to remember exactly where Duke's stall was and where the liveryman kept the saddles and bridles.

His knee banged painfully against a wheelbarrow full of manure, and he grunted. The inside of the livery was as dark as a crypt, and he knew he had to have light. He reached into his pocket for a match and scratched it on the heel of his boot. The match flickered, then caught fire. He held it up to reveal the interior of the cavernous barn. One glance reminded him that Duke's stall was the third on the right and that his saddle and gear were resting close.

"Duke" he whispered, edging forward toward the big horse. "Damn, it is good to see you again, boy. It's—"

"Freeze, Gunsmith!"

Clint froze because a gun was jammed into his ribs.

"Lift your hands. Lift them high!"

"Phil?" He had been in jail long enough to recognize the deputy's voice.

"That's right. And catching you is going to mean a lot to the sheriff."

He lifted his hands as ordered, but now the match was beginning to burn his fingers. Suddenly, it was burning and Clint gritted his teeth. Then he crushed the fire out with his bare fingers.

The room was plunged into darkness, but Phil jammed his gun even harder into Clint's ribs, grabbed him by the shoulder, and spun him around in the direction of the doorway. "One false move, just one, and you are a dead man. I don't need light to know that I can drill you."

Clint moved toward the door, saying, "No, I don't suppose you do."

When he reached the barn door, he said loud enough for Jenny to hear, "I guess I really walked right into your trap."

"You sure did, and if John didn't want to kill you personally, I'd put a bullet through you right now and be done with it."

Clint stepped through the doorway, and then he heard a scream as Jenny drove a pitchfork between them and its tines stabbed into the deputy's arm.

Clint spun and chopped downward. The deputy's gun went flying. "Get it, Jenny!" he said as he drove a looping uppercut to the deputy's jaw that sent him staggering against the barn.

Phil bounced off the wall and lunged with outstretched arms, but Clint planted his feet solidly and caught the man with a left cross that dropped him to his knees. The deputy started to shout for help, but Clint's boot caught him under the jaw, snapped him over backward, and knocked him out cold.

"Nice work, Jenny. I am sure glad you knew how to use a pitchfork. Couldn't have missed my back by more than an inch or two."

"What if he wakes up and spreads the alarm before we can saddle a couple of horses?"

Clint did not think that the man would revive for several hours, but it did not hurt to be sure. He gagged the deputy, tied him up with baling wire, then dragged him inside, and used the pitchfork to cover him up with a pile of dirty straw. With any luck, the man would not be found until morning when a stableboy came in and started mucking out the stalls and filling them with fresh straw.

He quickly saddled Duke and then chose a horse and saddle for Jenny Neal. "This adds horse stealing to the charges already on our heads," he told her. "Sure you want to come along?"

"What choice do I have? Phil will tell John that I helped you. I will be charged with that, plus my role in the jailbreak. I don't see that horse stealing can get me in more trouble than I am in already."

"Good point," Clint said. "But don't worry. When I find that stuttering girl, we'll come back and pay a little visit to the judge—just the three of us. He'll have to drop the charges against both of us when he hears the whole story. Besides, he has to be pretty worried about John Rankin turning on him. Rankin must be the one who killed O'Ginty or ordered him killed. The judge must realize that as much as we do. Unless I am sadly mistaken, Judge Wilson is probably damned eager to figure out a way to topple a sheriff who has already murdered one man and may start turning on others."

"Do you think the judge himself was a part of this whole rotten mess?"

"No. But have you ever thought that maybe John Rankin and his deputies set up that bank job, knowing your late husband would be all alone?"

"But why?"

Clint finished tightening the cinches, and now they were ready to ride. "Jenny, for a girl as bright as you seem to be, the answer to that question should be very obvious. John Rankin saw your husband as having what he wanted—the job of sheriff and the most beautiful woman in Arizona. Either one of those things would be enough motivation for murder. And there is one other thing."

"The bank's money."

"Yes," Clint said. "How much did they get away with?"

"Four thousand dollars."

"That's not bad."

He helped her into the saddle. "This entire thing is twisting around and around like a snake. The only question I can begin to find an answer to is who killed Sean O'Ginty. He must have known that Rankin or his deputies would want to eliminate him so that he could not testify on my behalf. Thus warned, he would have been prepared."

"Then whoever did it must have been someone he trusted!"

"Exactly," Clint said. "And that is what has me worried. There is a wild card running loose somewhere, and if O'Ginty couldn't see it before it killed him, then I might not either."

They rode out into the night, turned their horses

north, and raced through the back streets and out into the desert. Clint let Duke run for almost three miles before he eased him into a trot and angled back toward the main stage route to Phoenix.

It was a fine night, warm and glittering with stars. With such a beautiful woman riding at his side, Clint should have felt in good spirits, but he did not. In Phoenix, the Legend Maker would try to make him honor that damned contract before he revealed who the stuttering woman really was. Clint was not sure how he was going to handle Oscar Marsh—if the man could be handled at all.

And behind him in Tucson, there was a nest full of vipers to be cleaned out, and among them was a shadowy figure, someone beyond suspicion, whom O'Ginty had trusted enough to let his guard down.

Clint frowned. Sometimes a man could not be blamed for wanting to run away from his troubles. And I would do that, Clint thought, but I'm not quite ready to become a wanted man.

SEVENTEEN

Phoenix was founded about 1867 by a prospector named Jack Swilling who thought that a settlement in the Salt River Valley would be an ideal farming location. The town was named after the beautiful, mythical bird that consumed itself but rose from its own ashes and grew to become the symbol of immortality.

Jack Swilling and the other far-sighted land promoters and town builders who came there were well on their way to realizing their dream by the time Clint and Jenny arrived. Phoenix, though hellish in the summertime, proved to be well located, and when the desert was irrigated by canals, it blossomed.

It had taken Clint and Jenny two hard days of riding to get there, and when they checked into the best hotel in town, Clint was mighty glad that Jenny had thought to bring some money, for he was flat broke. They ate an early dinner, and then while Jenny prepared to retire, Clint took a bath and changed into clean clothes. He did not know where he was supposed to find the Legend Maker, but he guessed the man would most likely be hanging around one of the better saloons.

Phoenix was small enough to cover in an evening, and after Clint had strolled through several saloons, he finally spotted Oscar Marsh. The man was totally engrossed in conversation with two rough gunmen whom Clint did not recognize.

For a moment, he hesitated, wondering if it would be better to wait until morning to confront Oscar; with a shake of his head, he decided that he wanted to get this bit of unpleasantness over with as quickly as possible.

"Evening, Oscar," he said, "don't want to interrupt you men, but—"

"Gunsmith! Well, am I glad to see you here! Grab a chair and sit right down! We got business to discuss. Money to make!"

"Uh-uh," Clint said, not failing to notice how the two gunmen seemed to stiffen at the mention of his name. "All I want to do is find the girl who learned to stutter."

Now, the broad smile on Oscar Marsh's face melted, and he pursed his lips. "That does pose a real dilemma for us all. You see, this is Waco Jones and that is Texas Bob Hadley. I know you have heard of them."

Clint stepped back, making sure his gun hand was free and easy by his side. "Yeah, I've heard of them. Wanted for murder and robbery, aren't they?"

Waco Jones stood up. "Me and Texas Bob, we served our time in prison and we just been paroled. You got a problem with that, Gunsmith?"

"No. Just as long as you, him, and me stay away from each other, we'll get along just dandy."

"Boys, boys! We are all working for the same outfit here! My Great Wild West Outlaws and Gunfighters Show is going to make us all rich this coming year. We got to work together, not fight among ourselves! Clint, I told you that the audiences like action. Well, these are the boys who are going to give it to you."

"What is that supposed to mean?"

"That we stage a fight, a real honest-to-God saloon brawl with chairs and bottles and teeth flying and—"

"Now wait just a damn minute!"

"No," Oscar said, "you listen to me. I knew you'd be here and I feel damned lucky to have latched on to these two famous outlaws to balance our act. I know that the four of us can come up with a great performance, and I want to stage the first one right here in Phoenix on Saturday night!"

Clint shook his head. "You must be completely loco," he growled. "If you think that I am going to take on this pair of—"

The outlaws shoved back their chairs and stood with their hands poised by their guns. "I'd be real careful what you say next," Texas Bob said in a soft, deadly drawl. "You damn sure ain't fast enough to take the both of us."

Waco Jones was the bigger of the pair, and he ignored the commotion in the saloon as men dived under the tables. He backed up his friend. "I don't like lawmen," he drawled. "In fact, I hate them."

"I am an ex-lawman," Clint said, deciding that he would put a bullet into Waco first and then try to get his second shot into Texas Bob before the man cleared leather. "But don't let that stop you."

"Boys!" Oscar Marsh wailed. "Boys! This is no way to start our partnership."

"We don't need him," Waco hissed.

"That's right," Texas Bob added. "We'll just eliminate the gunfighter part of the show right now and you can pay his wages to the outlaws!"

"No!" Oscar shouted, pushing between them with an uncharacteristic display of reckless courage. "We do this my way or not at all!"

"Then not at all," Clint said. "You just tell me where you stashed that stuttering girl, and I'll ride on back to Tucson tomorrow and get everything straightened out."

"Stuttering girl? I really don't know who you are talking about."

Clint grabbed him by his shirt and hauled him up onto the tips of his toes. "Listen, damn you, I went to see Lola, and she told me all about the woman named Sherry who went away with you before I could get a chance to talk to her. Now, where is she!''

Sweat beaded across Oscar's fat, round face, but he shook his head and sputtered, "You kill me in front of everyone here, you'll hang, Gunsmith. And I'm not going to tell you anything until we do a Saturday night show. I'm broke, damn it! We all need money! I can't pay any of you until we sell some tickets!''

Clint dropped him. Both Texas Bob and Waco had drawn iron and had their guns leveled on his stomach. That made Clint go cold inside with a fury that he could barely contain. But he had learned from watching others die that a man's temper often was his ticket to the graveyard.

"All right," he said, stepping back, "we'll do a show. One show! Then you are going to tell me who that girl is so that I can take her back to Tucson and get my name cleared.''

"What about Sheriff Rankin? Do you think that he and his deputies are going to let you waltz back into their town and explain everything? You've got the sheriff's woman with you, isn't that true?''

"That's my problem," Clint said. Ignoring the two outlaws, he pulled up a chair and sat down. "Now, let's hear about this show you fellas were cooking up when I walked in.''

Waco Jones and Texas Bob exchanged brooding glances and finally the latter nodded. They sat down and poured whiskey all around, and as they did, the other patrons of the saloon picked themselves off the floor and crawled back up to the tables and the bar. A couple of minutes later, the piano player was coaxed back to his seat and began to thump out a tune.

Clint didn't ask to take one of Oscar's cigars. He

reached out and plucked one from the man's pocket, bit off the tip, and lit it. Inhaling deeply, he stared at the trio surrounding him.

Damn if this wasn't the sorriest lot he had ever taken up with!

EIGHTEEN

It was supposed to be a skit. At the time they had come up with it and then worked out all the fine details, Clint had not been happy. Now, as showtime approached, he was even less happy. But it was too late to back out. The Gunsmith had reluctantly given his handshake on the deal and he was going through with it.

Clint peered through the curtains into the big hall that also had a stage and was used by a traveling theater. The place was filling up fast, and at two dollars a head, it figured that his one-third of the gate split might even come to the hundred that Oscar Marsh had promised.

One thing for sure, the promoter knew his business. He had ordered handbills printed up and tacked all over town proclaiming that the Gunsmith was going to have a real gunfight with the notorious outlaws Texas Bob Hadley and Waco Jones. It was not to the death, nor even with real bullets, but all the same, with special blank cartridges that would demonstrate the true speed of a legend. It was, the bill advertised, to be one of the most thrilling confrontations ever staged in the West.

Clint had been apprehensive about the idea from the very beginning and had privately insisted to Oscar Marsh that, while the gun on his right hip would be filled with blanks, a second weapon on his opposite hip was going to be loaded. He simply did not trust the two outlaws, nor did he feel safe going up before an audience without being armed. He had killed too many men to take the chance that one of their friends or relatives might buy a ticket with the sole idea of killing an unarmed gunsmith.

"Ladies and gentlemen!" the Legend Maker cried out. "It brings me immense pleasure to present to you The Great Wild West Outlaws and Gunfighters Show."

If the man expected applause, he was in for a disappointment because the only sound was some drunk in the back who yelled, "Aw, let's get on with the show, you overstuffed bozo!"

The audience laughed and Oscar smiled as if he had just received life's greatest compliment. "As you may or may not know," he began, his voice suddenly becoming very serious and somehow filled with urgency, "what is going to happen on stage is completely unrehearsed and promises to be so thrilling that it will be talked about for years. Rather than introducing the stars of this show, I prefer to let them come out and introduce themselves. First, the outlaws, Waco Jones and Texas Bob Hadley, both just released from serving twenty-five years in the Texas State Penitentiary where they killed ten prisoners each with their bare hands!"

Clint groaned, but the audience loved it; whooping and howling, they stomped the floor with their boots and it was plain that they were in a hell-raising frame of mind and probably hoping the outlaws would tear the Gunsmith apart or fill him full of hot lead.

The pair sauntered out with exaggerated swaggers and both men looked tough enough to eat a boxful of horseshoes. They were smoking Oscar's long cigars, and with their black hats and red bandannas, they were quite a picture.

"I'm Waco, and any sonofabitch in the house who thinks he's man enough to wind my clock can step the hell up on this stage and give 'er a try. I like to gouge out eyeballs and bite off ears, and the sight of human misery makes me happy. I killed sixteen men before my twentieth birthday, and that don't count the greasers, coloreds, and Indians. I never met a man I liked, and I aim to tear the Gunsmith's head off tonight and throw it at you!''

The audience gaped in disbelief. No one was smiling now. Clint took a deep breath and wished he were anywhere but in Phoenix. Waco snapped a glance at him standing in the wings and spat tobacco on the floor. If this were an act, Clint had to admit he was as fooled as anyone in the room—Waco wasn't kidding!

When no one said anything, Waco spat again and then took a step back and let his friend take the center of the stage.

"I'm Texas Bob Hadley, and where I come from, if a man smiles, we rip his lips off and feed them to our dogs. I hate lawmen worse than scorpions and horse-flies. A lawman like the Gunsmith killed my daddy when I was twelve years old, and I tracked the sonofobitch down, shot his balls off, then tied him face down over an anthill. I am the fastest man alive with a gun or a knife, and there ain't no such thing as being second fastest—not in this world there ain't. I been killin' sheriffs and Texas Rangers for five years, and it is getting to be so borin' that I figured I would like to kill someone famous so that I'll be famous. The best that could be found on short notice was the Gunsmith, but he ain't nothing but a has-been. I aim to do some work on him tonight. Anybody think I'm just braggin'?''

Texas Bob's eyes pinned every man in the crowd, and no one so much as met his eye. ''All right you bunch of chickens, then I got to turn this over to the man who only has a few minutes left to live.''

Clint swallowed dryly. Both the outlaws had been more than convincing, and even Oscar looked mighty worried as he cleared his throat and struggled to keep his voice calm. "Well, folks, as you can see for yourselves, my outlaws are rough and tough fellas who promise to be quite a challenge to the Gunsmith. Frankly, I would not take ten thousand dollars to be in his shoes this evening, would you?"

"Nooooo," the crowd responded in unison, most men shaking their heads emphatically.

"Well, folks, that is why the Gunsmith is a legend and we are just mere mortals. So let's give a real warm welcome to the greatest living gunfighter in the west. Gunsmith!"

The audience applauded but not too loud, for Waco and Texas Bob were still on stage and glaring out at them as if taking notes to be used later.

Clint took a deep breath and moved out onto the stage, and when the last man finished clapping, he said, "I am not a man who has ever said much about what I did or did not do. I never killed anyone who didn't need killing, and even then I hated to do it, much preferring to arrest and let the law serve out fair justice."

He paused. "But sometimes, men did not wish to wait for rope justice, knowing their crimes were so evil that they would surely swing. On such occasions, they would challenge and draw on me, and understanding that they wanted to die and deserved to die, I killed them cleanly."

Clint toed the stage. "I do not know exactly how many men I have actually killed, but every one of them troubled me afterward. I am, and I say this humbly, blessed and cursed with my ability to draw faster than any man I have ever met, and I have learned to shoot with great accuracy. Many men have doubted this was true, and some died for their curiosity.

"I hope," he said, looking right into the eyes of Waco and Texas Bob, "that this is not the case of things this evening. That is all I have to say."

The Legend Maker nodded. "That was as fine and as humble a speech, ladies and gentlemen, as you will ever hear from a legendary gunfighter. Now, before our dramatic reproduction of an actual gunfight, I give you the chance to ask these famous men any questions that you have in mind. As for my own thoughts, I find it especially heartening that the Gunsmith is, despite his fame, a man filled with genuine, I mean really genuine, humility. I remember when I met Billy the Kid. He was so arrogant, and the Earp brothers, they—"

"Aw, shut up, and let us ask them the questions! Damn bozo!"

This time, Oscar Marsh colored with anger. He nodded his head stiffly and stepped back. "First question!"

"Gunsmith, how many men did you say you killed?"

"I said I didn't know and I never wanted to keep count."

"Then you don't put notches on the butt of your gun?"

"Only a showoff or a fake would do such a stupid thing."

"Gunsmith, who was the meanest man you ever killed?"

He had to think about that a minute. "The one who comes first to mind as being the most deserving to die by my gun was named Red Taggert. He and his band of equally cold-blooded murderers cut themselves quite a no man's land outside of Yuma. I'm sure a lot of you remember his cursed name."

There was a general nodding of heads. "More questions?"

"Are you the fastest gun who ever lived?"

Clint thought about it for a moment before answering as truthfully as he could. "I don't know. And as long as I never meet one faster, I do not care."

This caused a ripple of laughter until Texas Bob said, "That happens tonight!"

Clint glanced over at the man and saw both he and Waco were seething because no one had bothered to ask them any questions. "Maybe someone in the audience has a question for the outlaws," he said hopefully.

There were no questions, probably because no one dared to ask them. Clint shook his head. That was a very bad sign and it left him with a sense of foreboding. Clint had a strong hunch that Waco and Texas Bob were both itching to make their own legends this evening —entirely at his expense.

NINETEEN

The curtains were drawn for a moment while a poker table and chairs were placed in the center of the stage. The table was complete with chips and a deck of cards. A flimsy makeshift bar that Clint and Oscar had quickly hammered together out of packing crates was dragged out, and glasses and bottles were readied to make the set resemble a saloon. They had also found a piano and a player.

"All right," Oscar said, his face flushed with exertion as well as excitement. "We have carefully rehearsed all the lines. Remember, the argument builds until you, Waco, throw the first punch. I will slap my hands together and it will sound—and appear—as if you have really belted the Gunsmith. He will fake a fall, then crawl to his feet, and hit you back, only like before, it will be all fake just as we practiced. From out in the audience, it will sound and look so real that they will wince."

"What is the cue to the gunfight?" Texas Bob asked with a cold smile.

"The cue is when Clint says, Fill your hands, you mangy outlaws!"

Clint scowled. "Why can't I just say something like, Draw!?"

"Because that would not be dramatic enough. This is the stage! The theater! This is nothing less than your historic debut. This could be—"

"Never mind," Clint interrupted wearily. "Let's just get this over with and collect our money. Then I want the stuttering girl's name as you promised. After that, Miss Neal and I are riding back to Tucson."

Oscar looked grieved, but he nodded. "Perhaps the magic of stage fever will touch your heart, and you might have a change of mind. Who knows what will happen?"

Clint glanced at Texas Bob and Waco. "That's what I have been asking myself and not liking the answers," he said grimly. "Maybe you ought to talk to them again and remind them that this is supposed to be a skit, a performance, to earn money. It's not a war or an opportunity to kill me and become famous."

"I am sure they understand that if they . . . misbehave, shall I say, they will not be paid."

"That does not greatly comfort me," Clint growled as he took his place beside the flimsy little bar. "Let's get this over with."

When the curtain came up, the audience leaned forward. The piano player began to play "Buffalo Gal," and suddenly the scene was as real as many of the tent saloons that sprang up in hundreds of boom towns across the west.

Clint was leaning against the bar, and now he had to give his opening line to Oscar, who played the bartender. "I sure would like to shoot me a couple of outlaws this evening," he yelled loud enough for the paying customers in the back row to hear. "My friend Dudley the mortician has a wife and eight kids to feed, and I haven't been sending him near as much business as he needs lately."

"Maybe things will pick up, Gunsmith," Oscar bellowed with sympathy.

"Sure hope so, for Dudley's sake and the sake of his kids. I just hate outlaws. If I don't shoot at least a couple a day, I feel as if I didn't earn my pay."

At that, Waco threw his poker hand down, scraped his chair around, and stood up. "You be a famous lawman?"

Clint nodded. "That's right. You be a famous outlaw?"

"That's right! My name is Waco Jones and my friend here is Texas Bob Hadley."

The piano player slammed both fists down on the keyboard with a dramatic effect and then threw himself off the stage. For his own part, Clint acted shocked because the names were so famous. Oscar poured him a drink of whiskey, somehow making the neck of the bottle tinkle like a bell on the glass to show how nervous he, too, was at hearing such famous outlaws were in the same room with the Gunsmith.

Waco snarled. "Before me and my good friend ventilate you, Gunsmith, I think we ought to have a final drink together. What do you say?"

"I think that sounds just fine."

The two men came to the bar and Oscar poured three tall glasses of whiskey.

"To dying!" Waco hissed.

"To dying," they all toasted before drinking the whiskey down neat. It was such terrible whiskey that it brought tears to Clint's eyes, and when he blinked, he saw Waco's fist coming right at his face.

Oscar dropped his hands behind the bar and slapped them together, but he needn't have because Waco's knuckles connected with Clint's jaw with enough force to send him crashing over the bar, collapsing it in a pile.

Oscar shouted but neither of his outlaws paid him one damned bit of attention. They had already forgotten their lines, and it was pretty damned certain the play was over and their real fun was just beginning.

Waco pulled Clint to his feet and drew back his fist, but Clint managed to block the punch and drive a knee into his testicles. That doubled the man up and dropped him to roll around in agony. The audience howled with delight, thinking this was wonderful acting.

It wasn't. Texas Bob struck twice—so fast and hard Clint's head rocked one way and then the other. Clint grabbed on and then slammed his boot down on the man's toe. When he broke his bear hug, Clint smashed him in the face and Texas Bob staggered. He grabbed a bottle of whiskey out of Oscar's hand and tried to scramble Clint's brains. He missed, and when he lost his balance, Clint punched him in the ear. The man spun halfway around.

"Get up, you two," Clint breathed, feeling his blood pound, "and let's give this crowd a real show!"

They came to their feet. Both men dropped their hands over their guns. Clint stared at them and then he remembered his line. "Fill your hands, you mangy outlaws!"

They both grinned murderously, looked at each other, and then nodded. That was when Clint knew that they had substituted the blank cartridges they were supposed to be firing for real ones. They were going to kill him!

Clint understood with dead certainty that Texas Bob was fast, too fast for him to beat with a draw to the gun on his left hip. There seemed only one hope, so Clint's hand flashed for the harmless gun on his right hip. When he brought his Colt up, he leveled it at their faces and pulled the trigger.

There was a blast and smoke. The distance was so close that their beards were pelfed by flecks of gunpowder and instantly caught on fire. They bellowed helplessly and Clint used that moment to pistol-whip them both. When they crashed to the stage, he turned, bowed to the crowd, and then waved.

The audience, momentarily stunned by the sudden violence and the realism of the action, now seemed to waken as if from a trance. They rose to their feet as one and lustily cheered the Gunsmith. They stomped their feet, howled with delight, and threw money on the stage. "Curtain! Curtain!" the Legend Maker shouted almost hysterically.

The curtain fell as Oscar and Clint both reached for a bottle of whiskey. It was the most exciting act either of them had ever witnessed in their lives.

And for Clint, it was his first and last stage performance.

TWENTY

The first thing that Clint did was to take the guns away from Texas Bob and Waco. Then he made sure they were on their way out of town. He left them at the outskirts of the city and he pitched their empty guns on the road.

"You are both lucky to be alive," he called to them.

It was dark, but even so, Clint could see that their faces were a mess of burned whiskers and blisters. It must have hurt them both plenty just to speak, but somehow Waco did as he crawled off his horse and retrieved their empty weapons.

"You ain't seen the last of us, Gunsmith. You'll pay for what you did to Texas Bob and me in front of all those people!"

"Why don't you both ride back to Texas and take up a new line of work?" Clint suggested. "Go into farming or something like that where you might live to see old age."

"Nosiree!" Texas Bob hissed through blackened and blistered lips. "We'll be waiting for you down in Tucson when you come back. We figure that sheriff down there might just welcome a little extra insurance."

Clint bit down hard, trying to control his anger at Oscar Marsh who had to have told them of his intentions. The last thing he needed was for these two blood-thirsty and revenge-crazed bastards to be standing alongside Sheriff Rankin and his crowd of deputies, waiting to see who downed the Gunsmith first.

119

"I ought to kill you now," he said, "and save myself the trouble later."

"Yeah," Waco agreed, "but you can't because you ain't like us. You're soft, Gunsmith. You never learned that things like honor don't stand up to a bullet. It's going to get you killed down in Tucson—bet on it!"

Clint had nothing to say to that. He reined Duke around and headed back to town. It was almost midnight, and when he finished bedding Duke down, he started for his hotel. Jenny Neal would have heard about the stage performance, and she would be eager to see him. That would be just fine, he thought as he took the stairs two at a time and then started down the hallway.

"Clint?" a voice called softly.

He stopped and drew his gun as he saw a figure shrouded in shadow standing just a few feet inside the room. Recognizing the shape of a woman, he holstered his weapon and stepped forward. "Who is it?"

"An old friend," she whispered seductively as she moved forward. "I thought it was time you and I had a reunion. A very physical reunion."

"Sherry?"

"Y–y–yeah!"

"It is you!" Clint grinned and stepped inside, closing the door. The light was poor, but he could see her clearly. She was tall and perfectly shaped, a real love goddess with all the right curves and creases. "I ought to be damned mad at you for getting me into so much trouble, but the truth is," he said, remembering how terrific she had been in bed, "the truth is I never can stay mad at a pretty woman for very long."

She laughed and slipped off her dress, and he stared at that lovely figure of womanhood and it filled him with desire. She moved up to him and began to unbuckle his gunbelt. When she slid her fingers into his pants and began to make him stiff with a need for her, Sherry giggled and said, "Why don't you punish me, Gunsmith? Punish me with this." She dropped down to her knees and took him into her mouth. He groaned with pleasure.

"You're the one I've been hunting for all right, honey. You have a style all your own."

"Hmmm," she cooed as he reached down and began to fondle her proud breasts. "Gunsmith, you taste just won . . . der . . . ful!"

"Gunsmith, darling?"

He was pulling on his boots and getting ready to leave. "What?"

Sherry sat up in bed, not bothering to cover herself, and Clint watched her light a cigarette. "I know that I got you into a lot of trouble, but neither I nor Sean O'Ginty ever expected all this to come out of it. I really liked Sean, and when I heard he was murdered, I left town on the run with Mr. Marsh. You see, Sheriff Rankin wouldn't hesitate to kill him or me."

"I'll protect you."

"I am sure that you can, but all the same, I just found a good job here in Phoenix, a respectable one even, working at a steak house where I earn pretty good tips. If I leave, I'll lose that job."

"I need you to tell the judge what happened."

"But what if he doesn't believe me, Clint? In Phoenix, I was just another prostitute. Why don't you make Oscar Marsh go before the judge and tell him what happened?"

"He didn't come into it until after O'Ginty was murdered, did he?"

"No."

"Then I still need you."

Sherry thought about it for a long, long time, and then said, "I don't understand why you just can't put it all in your past. We don't have to go back to Tucson."

"I do. I was almost starved to death by Sheriff Rankin, and I want that man's badge before he murders more people like Sean O'Ginty. O'Ginty tricked me, but I liked him all the same, and after our fight, I reckoned the score was settled. He didn't deserve to be murdered. Sherry, if you won't come back to Tucson for me, then do it for him."

Her eyes glistened. Her face was beginning to show the signs of age and hard living, but her mouth was generous and forgiving, and her eyes had a softness not often found among prostitutes. Clint could not help but wonder where her life had gone wrong to bring her into that line of work. Maybe here in Phoenix she could get a fresh start and find some happiness. She was still damned good-looking, and there was none better in the sack. Coupled with a good man, she would pull her share of the load and then some.

"All right," she reluctantly decided. "Is that Neal woman coming too?"

"Yes, and her life will be in at least as much danger as yours."

Sherry shook her head. "I just hope you are as good as you think you are with a gun, or you'll have two dead women on your conscience."

Clint buckled on his gunbelt. "Right now," he said, "I have two very beautiful and very much alive women who have more pressing needs."

Sherry giggled. "Bet she isn't as good as me."

Clint winked. "Nobody is, Sherry, but don't tell her I said that."

"What kind of a woman do you take me for?"

He reached out and fondled a breast and watched its nipple grow hard. "I haven't the time or the energy to go into that right now."

"You dog, you," she said. "Bet you go across the hall and do it to her, too."

"Thanks for helping," Clint said, meaning it very sincerely. "Thanks for me and for Sean O'Ginty."

Her smile faded. "Good night, Gunsmith."

TWENTY-ONE

Clint finished saddling three horses and checking their hooves for stones; it was ten o'clock in the morning, and had he been returning to Tucson alone, he would have been twenty miles down the road by now. As it was, the sun was going to be unmercifully hot, and it would take them a good three days to reach Tucson. He was in an ill humor made worse by his agreeing to allow Oscar Marsh to buy him breakfast as a gesture of friendship; the man had not stopped bending his ear in the two hours since.

"Gunsmith," the easterner pleaded, "what do I have to do to make you change your mind about going back down to Tucson? Stay with me and we will make so much that in one year we can retire for life."

"No thanks," Clint said. "It was because of you that I almost got killed last night; Waco and Texas Bob aren't very forgiving men, and I'll have them to face as well as Rankin and his boys down south."

"But I gave you their shares of the ticket sales!"

"I appreciate that. Still doesn't change anything."

The Legend Maker wrung his hands. "Listen, Gunsmith, what if I . . . well, what if I went ahead of you and had a little talk with everyone down there?"

"What good would that do?"

"I don't know but . . ."

Clint finished inspecting the horses' feet and wiped the beaded sweat from his brow with a forearm. "I'll bet it is going to be a hundred and ten today. We're going to die out there. Think I will tie these horses to the back of a stage and buy us tickets.''

"Why don't you leave the horses here in Tucson?"

"I probably should," Clint mused, "but after being a lawman so long, I sort of feel naked when I don't have Duke around to get me out of trouble. If I go to Tucson on a stage, I might have to steal another man's horse, and I am in enough trouble already.''

"You really ought to ride down on the stage.''

Clint eyed the brassy orb of sun that burned fiercely. "I think we had better," he said, starting for the ticket office and figuring it was going to take most of his share of last evening's earnings to pay for three fares.

"Then I am going with you," Oscar declared, hurrying after him. "You are going to need some help!''

"It's a free country, but if you are doing it in hopes that I'll change my mind about starring in your show, you can save yourself the price of a ticket because I am not.''

"I understand that. But honor compells me to come along and help you out. Even you are no match for what awaits down there.''

Clint stopped and his anger and impatience melted. "Listen," he said quietly, "I tried to get Jenny to remain here because there is no need for her to take a risk. But Jenny is stubborn, and once she figured that Rankin may have set her ex-husband up for a murder, wild horses couldn't keep her here in Tucson. As for Sherry, I just need her to face Judge Wilson.''

Clint took a deep breath. "The only one who has no reason at all to get involved with things down there is you, Oscar. And to be real honest, I sure don't need you to worry about along with those two beautiful women.''

"Just a damned minute!" the eastern promoter blustered. "I am no coward, and it just might surprise you to learn that even though I am a tenderfoot and mostly hot air, I am entirely capable of defending myself.''

"With what?''

Oscar dug an empty .44 caliber derringer from his vest pocket. It had a pearl handle and Clint knew that it was extremely accurate up to about thirty feet.

"Nice gun. You ever have occasion to fire it?''

"No.''

"That's what I thought,'' Clint said. "So if you are coming with us, you should at least keep it loaded.''

"I'll go buy some bullets right now.''

"Do that,'' Clint said. "But before you come along, you should realize that this is not some skit or act that we have worked out. I intend to clear my name of all charges with the judge and then investigate and prove that John Rankin not only killed Sean O'Ginty, but also his former boss, Sheriff Neal.''

"How?''

"I don't know,'' the Gunsmith admitted, "but I will find a way.''

Clint watched the man head off to find some bullets, and he wondered if perhaps he shouldn't refuse to allow Oscar Marsh to come along. His offer to help, while its spirit of friendship was appreciated, might well prove to be a big mistake.

Knowing Oscar, Clint thought that objecting would not accomplish anything because Oscar was the kind of fool who barged ahead, did whatever he wanted to do, and the consequences be damned. That was fine in business maybe, but in some lines of work, it could be fatal.

The stagecoach left at noon and they were the only passengers going south. Clint eased back into the cushions of the seat and pulled his hat down over his eyes. "Ladies and Oscar," he said, "it is a long dusty road we are about to travel. Best thing you can do is to rest easy."

The two women eyed each other warily. They were a lot alike in bed, but not in any other respect that Clint could see. He had also detected a bit of jealousy between them over who got to sit next to him as opposed to the easterner. Jenny won out. She leaned her head against his shoulder while Sherry sat quite rigidly.

"Sherry," Oscar said, "would you like to play a little game of poker?"

"Sure. What kind?"

Oscar grinned lecherously. "Strip poker."

The woman laughed, and when Clint looked down at Miss Neal, she was fighting a smile of her own.

"Deal me in," Clint said, pushing his hat up from over his eyes. "It's too damned hot to be all dressed up anyway. Miss Neal, you interested?"

Her cheeks colored. "Of course not!"

"Suit yourself," Clint drawled, cutting the deck and winking at the fat little easterner. As the stage rolled out of Phoenix, it occurred to him this trip might not be so bad after all.

TWENTY-TWO

By the time they began to approach the outskirts of Tucson, Clint guessed the four of them had gotten to know each other pretty darn well. What surprised and amused him most was the obvious attachment that had formed between Sherry and the Legend Maker, Oscar Marsh. On the surface, you would think that the two had absolutely nothing in common: one a frontier prostitute, the other an eastern showman and small-time promoter with a big-time line of bull that he could and did spread a mile wide and a hundred miles long.

But they both had been raised in Cincinnati and almost in the same neighborhood. They could fondly recount parks and shops and favorite childhood places. And surprisingly, Sherry was a well-educated woman who had read most of the classics including those by Melville, Emerson, Hawthorne, and Shakespeare, accomplishments that greatly delighted and impressed the easterner. For hours they discussed their favorite novels and books of poetry, and it soon became clear that they were infatuated by each other.

That was fine with Clint. They seemed like the most illogical match in the world. She was taller than he and far better looking, yet both shared so many mutual interests and were very similar in attitudes and ambitions. Sherry was searching for something more than simple respectability. She wanted a small piece of history and a chance to become quite wealthy, exactly the things that Oscar Marsh seemed to desire.

Listening to them talk so animatedly for hours despite

the heat and the dust gave him an insight into both of them that he would not have otherwise gained. It reminded Clint that sometimes it is a mistake to label people as being this or that. Often a person misjudges another. If nothing else, he saw the facade slip away from Oscar Marsh to reveal the true man underneath, who was much better than the front he put before the world.

All that aside, Clint was a mighty worried man as they neared Tucson, for he knew he faced long odds. Not only would he have to convince the judge to drop all charges against him and an outstanding arrest warrant, but he would have to deal with Waco Jones, Texas Bob Hadley, Sheriff Rankin, and his bunch of cutthroat deputies. Clint was the kind of man who always tried to avoid gunplay whenever possible, but this time he could see little chance to settle things peaceably—not as long as Rankin was the prime murder suspect in the death of Sean O'Ginty.

It was late afternoon and he could see Tucson about five miles up ahead. He stuck his head out the window and called up to the driver, "This is where we get off!"

The man had already been told. Now, as he hauled in on the lines and brought the coach to a rocking halt, everything was ready. The horses were lathered and weary, but Clint figured that Duke would have at least a few days of rest before he was needed again, while the other horses would be staying in this town.

Clint tossed a silver dollar each to the driver and the shotgun guard and yelled, "Appreciate you not mentioning there were passengers aboard to anyone."

The driver nodded. "It's nobody's business but your own. Thanks and whatever you four are up to, good luck!"

"We will need a little of that," Jenny Neal called out.

They watched the stage roll away and saw how the dust swirled up on the dry road, leaving a trail of pale brown lifting into the sky all the way into town.

"What do we do now?"

Clint smiled. "Why don't we show this pair of lovebirds your tree house, Jenny? We need a place to hole up until dark."

"Tree house!" they echoed with disbelief.

Clint grinned. He knew that Oscar could never climb that rope up to the first branch even if he wanted, which he would not. Still, there was shade and concealment under those giant sycamore trees, so it was a good place to hide.

"What do you think of it?"

Oscar stared upward and squinted his eyes. "Oh, yes," he said without any enthusiasm whatsoever. "I do see a floor way up there through the leaves."

"That's it," Jenny said proudly. "It is about eighty feet straight up."

Sherry was not impressed either. "Looks to me like it is fit for nothing but eagles. I'm keeping my feet planted on solid ground."

Clint smiled. "We all are. I think by now we can assume that Sheriff Rankin will have pulled his guard away from Jenny's house and that we can hide there until this thing is over."

"What are we going to do first?" Jenny asked.

"Visit the judge."

"He won't listen to you." Jenny frowned. "Clint, take it from me. I know the man. It isn't that he is out and out crooked. It's just that he wouldn't dare do anything to cross the sheriff."

"I was afraid of that."

"I do have one idea," Jenny added. "If I can persuade Mayor Billings and our newspaper editor, Mr. Roberts, to come along and listen to the entire story, I don't see how even the judge could refuse to drop all charges against you—not if he intends to be reappointed by our city."

"Can you do that?"

"I think so. Yes," Jenny said emphatically. "They are both good friends and were deeply saddened by my husband's death. They said that if I ever needed help I should call on them."

Clint felt the first stirrings of hope building in his chest. "Then let's do that," he said. "You bring them to Judge Wilson's house and we will all be waiting. But be careful. I don't have to tell you what will happen to you if you are seen by the sheriff or his deputies."

"I'll go with her," Oscar hesitantly volunteered.

Clint nodded. "Then that is the way we will do it." He watched the sun dive into the eastern horizon. "We will wait another hour; then we move. It'll be mighty interesting to see if there is any justice left in this town."

"There is," Jenny said. "If there were not, I wouldn't have returned. There would not have been anything worth returning to."

Clint nodded. He just hoped she was right. If not, they were all going to be in a whole bunch of hot water.

TWENTY-THREE

It was nine o'clock that night by the time they left Jenny's house. Clint and Sherry made their way toward Judge Wilson's house, while Jenny and Oscar went in search of the mayor and the town's newspaper editor.

"There it is," Sherry said. "That is Judge Wilson's place."

The house was the finest on the street, a two-story Gothic home with a wide veranda and an overhead porch. Clint could see a stable out in the back attached to a servants' quarters. "The man must be doing all right."

They huddled down behind some bushes and peered in through the front window. "Damn!" Clint whispered, "he has company tonight."

Sherry's eyes widened. "And one of them is Herman Billings, the mayor! What will we do now?"

Clint shrugged. "Jenny and Oscar are just going to have to realize that the man is out tonight and come back here without him. I doubt we can find either of them now."

"I don't know where the editor lives," Sherry said, biting her lip. "Damn, why didn't the mayor stay home this evening?"

"You can ask him that when we break up their party," Clint said. "I just hope that Jenny and Oscar are smart enough not to go hunting for the man all over town."

"So what do we do now?"

132

"We wait right here for a while and see what happens next." Clint smiled. "You might also say a little prayer for our two friends."

Jenny Neal was not accustomed to sneaking about in her own hometown. She knew everyone and everyone knew and liked her. That was why it was so difficult to move around without being recognized. But she had come prepared. Her face was shrouded in an oversized bonnet, and though she did not need it for the warmth, a long coat that reached clear to the ground concealed her eye-catching figure.

"What time is it, Mr. Marsh?"

"Nine-thirty," Oscar replied. "You just asked me three minutes ago!"

"Where is the mayor tonight?" she said in anguish as they stared at the darkened and empty house.

"I don't know," Oscar said in a voice stretched thin with anxiety. "By God, the man could be downtown in a saloon, or over at Lola's Place, or at some civic meeting. How should I know?"

Jenny nodded and managed a smile. This easterner was clearly overwrought, and she wished he would put that damned little derringer back in his pocket before he accidentally shot her or himself. That was all that she needed on top of everything else that was stacked against them.

Jenny could feel herself perspiring heavily under the long, woolen coat. She wished this were over, wished her husband's recent death and everything that had gone wrong since had just been one long nightmare that was about to end. Maybe, she thought, this is just a bad dream, and I will awaken any minute and it will be over.

She pinched her wrist and it hurt enough to remind her that this was no dream. It was reality and she was back in Tucson where John Rankin was the law and the law took what it wanted. John had taken her as he might very well have taken Sherry, forcibly and without love. She hated him for that, and now as she felt her own gun buried deep in the pocket of her coat, she was determined that she would not surrender to John or anyone else again. She would rather fight and die.

The Gunsmith had given her the courage to tap this new source of determination. Funny, she had imagined that such a man would have to be hardened and very cold-blooded. She remembered her first surprise when she had taken a dare and glanced through the saloon window to see him, a tall, rather boyishly handsome man, and slender, almost exactly opposite the mental picture she had created of a typical gunfighter.

Jenny smiled, remembering how the window had mirrored her own surprise when their eyes had met just for an instant that day. Strange, she thought, how a fleeting glance like that can change your entire life. If Clint had not arrived, and their eyes had not touched and sparked something between them, he would have ridden on, and she might well have been broken by now and the wife of Sheriff John Rankin.

Jenny shuddered at the thought—at how close to this dark fate she had brushed! Married to Rankin, she would have been demeaned, degraded, and abused until her soul rotted, and she either killed herself or slipped down to his level of depravity. I owe my life and soul to the Gunsmith, she thought. Funny, that it should have been a man of the gun like her beloved former husband.

"What time is it, Mr. Marsh?"

"A quarter to ten. What are we going to do?"

"We'll go find Mr. Roberts, the newspaper editor, and bring him by here on our way to the judge's house. Perhaps our mayor will have returned by then."

The editor lived in a modest, three-room house only a block from his newspaper office, and they saw him through the filmy curtains. He was reading a copy of his own newspaper.

"Miss Neal!" he said, opening the door and allowing them inside. "What—"

"James," she interrupted, "this is my friend Mr. Oscar Marsh."

"Perhaps you have heard of my Great Wild West Outlaws and Gunfighter's Show, sir. I make it a point to call on the local newspapers and—"

"Please, Mr. Marsh," Jenny cried with exasperation, "this is not the time for promoting your show. We are under some urgency here!"

"Yes," Oscar said, "I momentarily forgot that we are in some slight difficulty. Forgive me."

The editor was a small man in his fifties, trim, and possessing quick, intelligent eyes that darted from one of them to the other.

Jenny explained the circumstances in a rush, and the editor understood at once since he had covered the trial in great detail and sold twice the usual number of copies to readers who hoped for some scandal and even a degree of sexual titillation at what had transpired between Jenny and the Gunsmith.

"So that is the reason we are here," Jenny said. "You know how obstinate the judge can be. That is why we hoped that when you heard the complete story, you might help us sway his opinion in the name of justice."

"Of course. There has been damned little of that in Tucson since your husband's tragic death. Allow me just a moment to find my shoes. I'll come with you."

Clint looked at his watch. "It's ten-thirty and the mayor shows no sign of leaving, even though everyone else did. I think we had better pay our respects right now."

Sherry nodded. "Whenever you are ready."

Clint stood up and took the woman's arm, knowing it would be better if they walked boldly up to the front door rather than tried to surprise the judge and the mayor.

They knocked on the front door and the judge peered through the peephole. Their eyes met not three inches apart, but somehow the judge recognized Clint and the man cried, "Oh, my God, it is him!"

He whirled and Clint saw him start to race down the hallway. So much for bold confrontations, Clint thought as he threw his shoulder again and again at the heavy oak door until he finally managed to break the lock and the door crashed open. His forward momentum carried him flying into the room, and when he hit the waxed hallway floor, he was like a duck landing on an icy pond. He slid with great speed into a clock that smashed over on him in a shower of glass, brass pendulums, and a painted wooden bird that would not shut the hell up.

"Don't move!" the judge cried, holding a gun pointed down at him.

Clint gritted his teeth. "I can't move! Get this damned thing off me!"

The judge shook his head. "This time you will not escape the arm of the law. Herman, go find the sheriff or one of his deputies and tell him that I have single-handedly captured the Gunsmith!"

Mayor Herman Billings nodded vigorously and jumped for the open doorway, but he sucked his over-sized stomach right up next to his backbone as Sherry's gun found his bellybutton.

"Hi, lover boy," she purred, "you remember me? Sherry from Lola's place? Of course, you do. I was your number one girl over there. How is your dear wife?"

The mayor nodded rapidly. "Fine. Just wonderful, Miss Sherry!"

"Good. She's a delightful lady. Now, we would like to have a talk, a nice little talk. Would you like to have a talk, lover boy?"

"Sure. Sure, that would be great!" Sweat was pouring off his forehead.

"I thought so! Now, help the judge pull that big old clock off my friend. Then we can all go sit together in the parlor where we can discuss everything in comfort."

The mayor glanced at the judge who lowered his pistol and reached for the clock. "Come on, Herman, give me a hand. Talking won't kill anybody, but that gun in her hand damn sure will."

TWENTY-FOUR

Clint looked at the editor, the mayor of Tucson, and the judge. He had carefully gone over what had occurred before his arrest, and then Sherry had backed it up with her own explanation of how she had been paid by Sean O'Ginty to impersonate a stuttering Miss Neal.

"So you see," Clint said, "I had no way of knowing. Suddenly, I discover that Miss Neal is not only a lovely and very respected lady, not only the wife of your former sheriff, but also the owner of a millinery store. My mistake was regrettable, and I have apologized."

Jenny smiled. "And I accepted that apology. I want no part of sending a man to the penitentiary for two years for such a minor misunderstanding."

The judge frowned. "But you filed charges."

"I had no choice! I was forced to bring them against Mr. Adams by our sheriff. John was insanely jealous of anyone who even looked at me. Besides that, he openly admitted that he thought he was faster on the draw than the Gunsmith."

The editor looked at the judge. "I have no legal background, but shouldn't this case be thrown out and the Gunsmith exonerated of all charges?"

"And what would my life be worth if I did that?" Judge Wilson said finally.

Clint interrupted. "Listen, I know you and every other law-abiding man in this city are opposed to gunfighting, but you must understand that sometimes it is necessary against men who listen to nothing else."

"I can send for a U.S. marshal," the judge said,

thinking out loud. "That would take care of it."

"For how long?" Clint demanded. "As long as the man stayed in town? And what, Judge Wilson, would your own life be worth when the marshal left Tucson, even for one day?"

"Very little." Judge Wilson kneaded his temples with his thumbs. "I have sworn to protect the laws of this state and country. If I give you free rein to confront Sheriff Rankin and his deputies, someone will be killed."

Mayor Billings had listened thoughtfully, but now he interceded. "And if you don't let the Gunsmith clean that pack of murderers and thieves out, then what? We, the law-abiding citizens of Tucson, might as well close shop and start all over again somewhere else. Only there would just be another John Rankin who'd come along to threaten and dictate how we live. And what if it's true that Rankin had O'Ginty killed and was behind the death of Jenny's husband?"

"That must be proved in a court of law!" the judge cried. "It simply is not enough just to make wild accusations or suppositions without foundation."

"I'll find a way to prove that John Rankin was behind that holdup," Clint vowed. "But I still need your word that I have immunity from the charges against me."

"You stole a good horse and saddle from Ned Warner," the editor said. "Ned is my typesetter and a fine man."

"Jenny needed it to get out of Tucson after helping me escape. You can tell Ned that I am sorry and that his horse and outfit are back."

"That ought to be good enough," the editor mused.

Mayor Billings cleared his throat. "I think it is time we all admitted the truth. This town is under Rankin's control. I may be the mayor, but I carry no authority, and you, Judge, you sentence men more severely than you should because of Sheriff Rankin.''

He was looking right at the judge, but the man did not offer an argument because everyone in the room knew it was true. What Clint had done would have received no more than a few weeks in jail, a small fine, and a reprimand in any other courtroom.

The editor rubbed his hands together. ''I think it is time I also shouldered some of the blame for what has been happening. An editor's job is to be the social conscience of a city, and I have been sadly remiss in that responsibility. In the next issue of my paper, right on the front page, I am going to begin a campaign to get John Rankin and his hired dogs kicked out of town.''

Clint shook his head. ''I sure wish you wouldn't do that, Mr. Roberts. I figure that is as good a way as I know to get your printing press and office burned to the ground and maybe yourself killed.''

''I can't remain silent any longer, damn it! At the very least allow me to print the true story of what transpired here tonight.''

Clint thought about it. If he went after Rankin and somehow managed to kill the man and his deputies, Judge Wilson would have to see that he was sentenced to hang or serve a lifetime sentence in prison. But, if he were minding his own business and the law came after him, that was another matter entirely—a matter of self-defense.

''All right, print your story,'' Clint said. ''But if you do that, I will need a place to defend myself in case they come for me—a place where I can hold off a small army and not be burned out.''

''The old adobe chapel,'' Jenny said, snapping her fingers together.

"Yeah," the mayor said, "that would be perfect! It was a Mexican church before the roof fell in and they built a bigger one."

"Where is this place?"

"Just about a half mile out on the eastern edge of town. It's even got a good well you can use," the editor said. "Walls are three-feet thick with shooting slots for rifle barrels."

Clint nodded. "Open field of fire?"

"Nothing but a few cactus and some scrubby clumps of sage out there. Not enough to hide an Apache."

"An Apache," Clint said, "can make himself so small he can run along behind a lizard and stay out of sight."

"Then it's settled," the mayor said.

Clint hooked his thumbs into his cartridge belt.

"Judge, what's your ruling on this?"

Judge Wilson walked to a cupboard and produced glasses and whiskey. "I say if you are attacked you have the right to defend yourself, but before you go after anyone for the murders of O'Ginty or Sheriff Neal, you must have proof. Otherwise, you are going to be wanted for murder and I would sentence you to hang by the neck until dead."

Oscar said something low under his breath that pretty well summed up everyone's feelings. The easterner raised his own glass for the first toast. "To the end of fear and tyranny in Tucson!"

They all drank to that. Oscar filled the glasses again without bothering to ask the judge's permission and lifted his high. "To the greatest gunfighter I have ever had the pleasure to know, to stand beside, and to defend with my life if need be."

Clint glanced at the easterner to see if he was playing his role of showman and grand orator again, but Oscar was very definitely serious. Clint downed his drink, feeling grateful that he had at least got this much of it sorted out. Now, he would have to find a way to convince the two women and Oscar that he could handle the impending trouble on his own.

The trouble was, the moment that they were left unprotected by his gun, they would be attacked by Rankin or his deputies and suffer for helping him.

Clint frowned. It was tough enough worrying about how to take care of himself, let alone three others who probably had never fired a gun at anyone.

TWENTY-FIVE

They had only one day to prepare the adobe chapel before the next newspaper issue came out, and Clint used it well. He was handy with tools, and with Oscar's help, he was quickly able to cover a part of the roof with some of the fallen rafters. Jenny and Sherry cleaned out the place and stocked it with provisions donated by the editor and the mayor. Clint was not in a cheerful mood because it was not his style to await attack or even a prolonged siege. All his law career, he had been a man who had initiated action, not waited for it to come his way.

Still, he had promised the judge that he would not force a confrontation with Rankin and his deputies, and he would keep his word. If they came out to face him, well, that was a different matter.

Sherry was the only one of them who would escape association with the Gunsmith by Rankin or his men, so she offered to be the informant. It was a dangerous task, but she seemed committed to help in the best way that she could.

"I can get a job at O'Ginty's Saloon. Dennis knows me and he probably owns the place now."

"Why do you say that?"

"Because he was Sean's kid brother. Didn't he ever tell you?"

"No," Clint said, "I had the feeling that he didn't like Sean."

"Aw, they argued constantly, but if you attacked one, then the other was sure to jump in and fight. Anyway, Dennis will hire me and I'll be fine. Either that, or I go back to work for Lola for a while."

"No!" Oscar Marsh practically shouted.

Sherry's face softened. "All right," she said, "if it really matters all that much to you."

Oscar, for perhaps the first time in his life, seemed to be almost at a loss for words. "Just be careful," he said in a thick voice before turning away.

Sherry winked at Jenny and Clint and then she whispered, "I think he really likes me."

"I think you're right," Clint said. "And be careful. If you hear what they are up to, then wait until dark before you ride out and tell us. I don't want you taking any unnecessary chances."

"I won't." She kissed the Gunsmith a quick good-bye on the cheek and then went to Oscar who was standing alone, looking too old, too fat, and too frail for this kind of thing. Clint saw her take the easterner's chubby hand in her own and then kiss it. She looked into his eyes and said something to him that only he could hear.

Oscar's narrow shoulders lifted and he straightened to his full height. He sucked in his gut and flashed her that winning smile that he possessed. And then, he did something that made Clint's throat tighten a little. He took off one of his diamond rings and placed it over Sherry's finger.

Clint and Jenny both turned away because they had each seen too much already.

"Clint?"

"Yeah?"

"If they get through this, those two are going to get married."

"They'll be quite a pair."

"Just like we could be," Jenny said, looking up at his face.

"I thought we had already covered this ground,"

Clint said, watching the end of another blistering day and seeing the first clouds lacing up with gold and salmon colors.

"There is still time to change your mind."

"I think we have more pressing things to worry about—things like how are we going to survive whatever Rankin sends our way."

"That is a strange way to put it," Jenny said. "You sound as if he won't come himself."

"I don't think he will—not unless he has to. Why should he?" Clint asked. "He has deputies and friends he can count on to do the dangerous work."

Jenny nodded. "My husband once said that John had some coyote. Yes, that is how he put it. He said that John Rankin had some coyote in him. What did he mean?"

"The coyote is just about the smartest wild animal on the frontier—smarter by far than a horse or even a domestic dog. You kill one of his kind with a rifle, he'll quickly learn the range of it and stay just outside. You trap or poison one of his pack, you had better try something else the next time because he will remember. And yet . . ."

"And yet what?" Jenny pressed.

"And yet they are savage fighters when cornered. They will whip and usually tear apart a dog almost twice their size. Most people hold them in contempt. They forget that that when somebody who understands wild animals says that a man has some coyote in him, it is as much of a compliment as an insult."

"I see. Other men are called wolves. Is that the same?"

Clint smiled. "Wolves are generally men who take advantage of women."

Jenny watched Sherry riding toward town as the

twilight settled over the desert. "Why don't you be my wolf tonight, Clint? I want to make you howl."

He slipped his hand around her waist. Oscar was a big boy. He would understand when they moved out of the chapel and spread their blankets under the stars.

Clint awoke at sunrise and moved back inside when he heard Oscar cussing. The man looked haggard and out of sorts as he tried to light a small fire to boil some water for coffee. He wasn't having much success.

"You need to start with small kindling," Clint said.

Oscar did his own version of a growl. "Sure, while you and Miss Respectability are out there writhing around in passion, I am supposed to—"

"Now, wait a minute," Clint snapped, grabbing the man by the collar and hauling him to his feet. "If you got a burr under your saddle blanket, let's pull it the hell out!"

Oscar's round little fists knotted and he struggled free. "Don't push me, Gunsmith! I don't care how tough and dangerous you are!"

Clint shook his head and decided that the man wasn't acting like himself and that getting angry right back would only make matters worse. He released Oscar, squatted by the fire, and dug out his knife. He then began whittling long slivers off the thick branches Oscar had been trying to fire. "What's really the matter, Oscar? Did I say or do something I shouldn't have?"

"Damn right you did!"

"I promise to get up first in the morning and make our coffee if that is why you are so upset this morning."

"Don't make fun of me!"

Clint struck a match to the wood shavings and reached for a canteen and the coffeepot. "All right," he said, growing increasingly impatient, "I won't do that either as long as we level with each other. What the hell is wrong with you this morning?"

The Legend Maker began to pace back and forth. "Well, I was lying awake last night and all of a sudden I remembered something."

"What?"

"Texas Bob and Waco. They saw me and Sherry together. It was before you arrived in Phoenix. We had made a deal and—"

Clint didn't wait to hear any more. He dropped the coffeepot and moved toward his saddle. Damn! No wonder Oscar was all upset! There was no way that the Gunsmith could have known that the two outlaws would recognize Sherry. But they most certainly would!

"I'm coming with you!" Oscar yelled.

Clint whirled. When he spoke, his voice had the cut of a whip. "No, you are not. You are going to stay right here and take care of Jenny Neal."

"But, Gunsmith, please! I lovd Sherry!"

"I know that. And because of it you would get us both killed."

He lowered his voice as he threw his saddle over Duke's broad back. "You are a very intelligent man, Oscar—as smart as any I have ever met. So use that intelligence right now and stay here like I am ordering you."

A small, tortured noise came from Oscar's throat and he clenched his fists at his sides. "I should have remembered!" he cried. "I should have remembered they saw me and Sherry together! But why didn't she remember?"

Clint looked down at the man almost with pity. "Who says she didn't?"

TWENTY-SIX

Sherry had to admit that going back into Tucson had her half scared. Two days earlier, she would never have believed she would risk her life for anyone or anything. But since meeting Oscar Marsh, something had changed.

I am crazy, she thought, as she moved toward O'Ginty's Saloon where she intended to seek out Dennis and perhaps talk him into letting her have a job singing and playing the piano; with all her childhood years of piano, Sherry knew she could easily outplay the ivory-pounder he employed now.

As Sherry moved down the boardwalk that evening, she was aware of the hungry stares of the men she passed. Many of them made lewd comments and Sherry hurried on past them. She recognized a few as former customers, and one of them tried to grab her, but she kicked him in the shins and made him howl to the great delight of his friends.

Sherry glanced at her reflection in the windows. I look like a whore, she thought, and even in a white wedding dress, I would still look like a whore. She felt her eyes sting a little, knowing it was true. It had always been that way for her. She had grown up too fast, had large breasts at thirteen, a woman's body with a child's innocence. Raped by an uncle at fourteen, she had been used by men all her life until she had learned to use them first.

But Oscar, he was different. Clint was different, too, in that he was decent and honest and really wanted to give as much pleasure as he took, but Oscar had won her heart. Why? She did not understand it herself. She was the woman who had always admired big, tough men, the rougher the better. Oscar was not big or tough and sometimes he grated on her nerves with his incessant talk. But he was so vulnerable, so basically sweet and afraid and . . . himself. That was why she loved him—loved him in spite of all his failings as a man and perhaps because of them. He made her feel like a lady, not a whore. Maybe it had something to do with his having to use his own oratorical talents as a whore used her body, to seduce men into doing things for his own gain.

Sherry approached O'Ginty's Saloon with a great deal of anxiety. She had liked and trusted Sean, though they hardly knew one another, but the story on Dennis was entirely different. He was said to be a mean and sadistic sort who raped, bruised, and hurt women for his kicks. Perhaps the years of being forced to work for his older brother had twisted him. Sherry did not know and she hoped she didn't have to become familiar enough with him to find out.

The loss of Sean hit her strongly the moment she passed inside the swinging doors, but no one could have sensed this as she smiled and waved at men she had serviced and had drunk with at Lola's. She swayed seductively past the tables, causing quite a stir because it was the saloon's policy that only a few girls were allowed to come inside, and those that did and hustled men had to give a share of their earnings to the house. Sherry would have worked here right from the beginning, but she sensed that Sean had not wanted that, so she had gone to Lola.

"Where is Dennis?" she called to an overworked bartender.

"Upstairs in the office."

Sherry had heard of that office on many occasions. Sean O'Ginty had liked to sneak Madam Lola's prettiest girls up there during the afternoon and make love to them on his huge oak desk. Always a man of good humor, Sean had loved joking about his desk work.

Sherry knocked at the door. She had never really cared for Dennis, and thus she was not at all certain if he would give her a job or help her find his brother's killer. He might have her pitched out on her ear. Then again, he might want to sample what his brother had found so delicious. Sherry could not begin to guess what the younger O'Ginty would do.

"Who is it?"

"Sherry."

A moment later the door opened. "Well," Dennis exclaimed, "like a ghost out of the past! What are you doing in town? Last I heard, you were in Phoenix."

Sherry passed inside and her eyes swept the room; it belonged to Dennis now, but it had Sean's personality stamped all over it. She forced a smile. "I like Tucson better. More action. I was hoping . . . well, you know, that I might be able to pick up where I left off."

Dennis was in his late twenties, slender, dark-haired, and narrow-faced. He raised his eyebrows and said, "Oh? Then why aren't you back at Lola's? I heard you were her best girl, that you were pretty choosy, and that your prices were tops. I am sure that you can find employment there again."

"Yeah," she told him, "I can, but I am looking for a new line of work."

He laughed. "Once a whore, Sherry, always a whore."

His words cut deep into her, for there was truth in them that could not be denied. "I was, ah, kind of thinking you might need another girl to work the floor.

You know, sing a few songs—I can even outplay that monkey you have down there on the piano. Dennis, I'd be good for business.''

He studied her closely. "How old are you, Sherry?"

Her cheeks burned, and though her first thought was to lie, she couldn't do it. "I am forty-one."

"That old!" he said, clucking his tongue sympathetically. "That is really old for your line of work. I'd guessed you were in your mid-thirties. You look good for your age, amazingly good."

"Thanks," she said in a brittle voice.

"Before I give you a job, though, I think I'd like to see what the rest of you looks like. If I like what I see and sample, I'll let you go back downstairs and sing a couple of songs."

She nodded stiffly and began to undress, feeling his eyes on her body, feeling his heat, and then hearing him draw in his breath as he saw her perfect breasts. Sherry tried not to think of how he would feel on her and in her. She tried to think of this young man as just another body she would use for her own profit.

But it was hard, damn it! And Oscar was to blame.

An hour later she half stumbled back down into the saloon and walked to the piano player. "You're being replaced for a couple of days," she said. "Why don't you go have a drink on the house and then go practice somewhere? Learn some new songs. You have talent, but you're too damn lazy."

The man glared at her. "Who said you were taking my place?"

"Dennis."

They both turned to see him coming down the stairs, and he was buttoning his pants. Sherry waved and he waved back at her, all smiles.

"You cheap slut!" the piano player hissed.

Sherry fingered the keyboard. "Slut, yes. Cheap, no. And I am a damn sight better piano player than you will ever be. Now leave me alone."

A tear fell on the piano keys, and she wiped it off, and then, taking a deep breath, she threw her head back and let out a wild Texas yell and began to sing in a clear but slightly throaty voice:

"Oh come along boys, and listen to my tale,
    I'll tell you of my troubles on the old
    Chisholm Trail, come a ti ya you-py, you-py
    ya, you-py ya, Come-a ti ya you-py, you-py
    ya!"

Waco Jones and Texas Bob Hadley heard that voice as they were sauntering along the boardwalk, and when they peeked inside and saw Sherry, they both halted in their tracks.

"It's her," Waco said with a slow grin. "It's the woman that was with the Legend Maker!"

"Then he's probably about somewhere and so is the Gunsmith," Texas Bob said. "Maybe we better go tell the sheriff that they are back."

"Uh-uh," Waco grunted. "Let's watch her tonight and find out where she goes after the saloon closes. Then we grab her and make her talk."

"That'll be a pleasure."

Waco licked his dry lips. "Yeah," he said, "bet that woman is even better in bed than on a piano stool."

"If she is, we are in for a good time," Texas Bob said, "a real good time!"

TWENTY-SEVEN

Clint did not race straight into Tucson, even though he would have liked to. Instead, he angled up the streets and down alleys until he reached the familiar back door of O'Ginty's Saloon. He tied Duke up and knocked, but there was no answer. He slipped up the alley and went in the front door.

It was not yet eight o'clock in the morning, but saloons never close. There were still a couple of drunk men at the bar though the poker and faro tables were empty. No one paid Clint any attention, and he passed them and then took the stairs two at a time. He was not even sure where Sherry was staying, but he did know that she had intended to try to go to work here for Dennis O'Ginty.

He pounded on the door, and when no one answered, he pushed his way inside. Dennis was sound asleep on the couch, his face puffy with sleep, a half-filled bottle of good Kentucky whiskey on the floor at his side.

Clint walked over and nudged the man. "Wake up, Dennis. I need to talk to you."

"Get outta here!"

"Wake up, it's the Gunsmith."

At the mention of the name, his eyes flew open, and they were bloodshot but wide with alarm. "What are you doing here?"

"I'm looking for Sherry."

He sat up too quickly and groaned. "She came in for a job last night. I auditioned her. She got the job and played the hell out of the piano. Gonna make me a lot of money."

"Where is she?" Clint did not care about how much money she could make for this man.

"How should I know? As long as she comes back and plays again tonight, what she does until then isn't my business."

"Listen," Clint said, trying to keep patient, "Sherry is here to help me find out who murdered your brother. We're pretty sure it was Sheriff Rankin and if she can just—"

"You think the sheriff was behind my brother's death?" Dennis interrupted with a look of disbelief.

"Yes. He had Sean killed so that the man couldn't help me testify in court."

"Well, I'll be damned! I thought he was probably robbed. Sean liked to carry a lot of money around with him. I always told him that it was a dangerous habit. He'd carry a couple hundred dollars even when he went over to Lola's or just out raising hell."

"Where did they find his body?"

"Out in the alley. No sign of any struggle."

"Was he armed?"

"He carried a derringer like most of us."

Clint frowned. "Was his wallet missing?"

"Sure. One of the deputies found it down by Peterson's General Store."

"Which deputy?"

"The one named Phil. Phil Blum is his name."

"I know him very well. Maybe I ought to have a talk with Phil."

"Maybe. But if I were you, I would get on my horse and ride the hell out of Tucson as fast as possible. Sheriff Rankin is after you, and once he holds a grudge, there is no stopping the man."

Clint wasn't really listening. The first thing he wanted to do was to find Sherry and send her on back to the adobe chapel where she would be out of danger. Then, he guessed he would locate Phil and try to squeeze out some information, perhaps even a confession for Judge Wilson.

"They got you on a charge of horse thieving, too," Dennis warned. "They catch you, you'll hang instead of going to the penitentiary."

Clint nodded and headed for the door. "Thanks for the warning," he said. "And if Sherry comes by early for any reason, I'd appreciate it if you'd bring her up here and keep her safe and out of sight until I come back."

Dennis managed a devilish smile. "I had her up here last night, and I'm plenty willing to do it all over again if it will help you out. For an older woman, she sure has got a fine body and knows how to use it."

Clint turned and left without comment. For some reason, he didn't like the younger O'Ginty, and since he was asking for the man's help, it was best he kept his mouth shut, but it was not easy.

He was not sure where to start hunting for Sherry, but he knew that he had to find her before she was spotted by Waco and Texas Bob.

Clint wanted to stay out of sight of the sheriff and his deputies, if at all possible. Besides, he figured that they would be coming for him soon enough and that the adobe chapel was the place to make his stand.

Because a lawman's busiest hours are after dark, they usually sleep late on quiet mornings, and Clint used this knowledge based on his own years of experience to move freely from one hotel to another until he found the one he was looking for.

"Yeah," the desk clerk said. "I sleep in the first room

at the top of the stairs when I am not down here in this damned lobby. This morning about two o'clock I was awakened by a hell of a ruckus. When I came to the door to see what was happening, I saw a woman matching the description you just gave me.''

"What was all the ruckus about?"

"Hell, the poor thing was being dragged into her room by two ornery looking sonsofabitches! I mean they were rough. I just closed and bolted my door and went back to bed."

"And you let them do that to her?"

"Hell, yes. In this business you learn to keep your mouth shut and your eyes wide open. If I had tried to interfere, they'd likely have killed me!"

"Describe them."

It took Clint about fifteen seconds to make sure that the two men were Texas Bob and Waco. Filled with an icy deadliness, Clint said, "Which room are they in?"

"Number 204. Upstairs, second door on the right."

"If they have killed her, I'm coming back down here to throw you right through that glass window."

The man blinked. His cheeks puffed out and he stammered, "Well—well, damn it! At least that way I'd have a chance of living! You bust in that room and you had better have your gun working fast!"

In answer, Clint drew his gun and started up the stairs. He was feeling a dread in the pit of his stomach, and he also felt a cold fury at having ever agreed to allow Sherry to come into town alone.

If Waco and Texas Bob had killed her . . . Clint shook his head . . . even if they had not killed her, it was showdown time and someone was going to get shot.

TWENTY-EIGHT

Clint tried to peer through the keyhole to 204, but he could see nothing. He stood outside the door debating his next move and not wanting to do anything foolish that might endanger Sherry's life even more than it already was. Finally, he just decided that he had no choice but to smash the door off its hinges and go in with his gun bucking in his fist.

With any luck, Waco and Texas Bob would be asleep at this early hour and not be able to reach their guns before he had the drop on them. At that point, it was up to them if they chose to live or die.

Clint lifted his leg and kicked out at the door just as hard as he could. The impact of his boot splintered wood, but the bolt held by just a fraction. That is where he lost that precious moment of surprise. By the time he could throw his shoulder back into the door and crash on into the room, Texas Bob had managed to grab his gun and pull Sherry up to shield his naked body. Waco was still sleepy, but when he saw Clint, he threw his hands up and cried, "Don't shoot me!"

Clint paid the man no attention during that first moment. His gun was pointing at a part of Texas Bob's face that he could see behind Sherry, and he knew at that instant that it would be too risky a shot and that the man had him cold.

"Drop your gun, or the woman gets the top of her skull blasted off," Texas Bob whispered. "Drop it, Gunsmith."

"Shoot!" Sherry cried, "go ahead and shoot or he'll kill us both anyway!"

"Shut up!" Texas Bob screamed. "Make up your mind, Gunsmith!"

Clint dropped his gun as he stared at Sherry. Her face was battered, both eyes purple and swollen, and her lips were smashed and caked with blood. She was naked and that lovely body of hers was covered with angry bruises and welts. They had obviously beaten the hell out of her last night and abused her horribly.

"Get his gun, Waco!"

The man bounced out of bed, scooped the gun up, and then whipped Clint across the cheek with its barrel. Clint felt warm blood course down his cheek and realized he had fallen to one knee.

"I'm going to kill him!" Waco hissed.

"No!"

"What do you mean?"

Texas Bob never took his eyes off Clint. "I mean that if we send for the sheriff, we can collect that reward and earn ourselves a nice favor in this town. If we kill him all by ourselves, we make the sheriff mad. So go get him, Waco. Get your clothes on and bring him here while I keep guard."

Waco was not happy. With a curse, he drove a meaty fist into the side of Clint's head that flattened him on the floor. "All right," he snarled, "but we share the reward."

"Sure. Now go find Sheriff Rankin."

Clint shook his head, trying to clear his mind. The two blows had left him dazed and unsteady, yet he knew that somehow he had to kill Texas Bob and get Sherry out of this hotel and back to the adobe before Rankin and his deputies came back. Clint gave himself about five minutes.

"You're finished, Gunsmith. Rankin hates you even more than I do. He's going to hog the pleasure of killing you."

"And get all the credit," Clint said thickly. "The man who kills the Gunsmith will be famous—famous enough to enable the Legend Maker to pay him a hundred dollars a week instead of me."

"That fat little bastard was going to pay you that much?"

"Sure," Clint said. "Hell, we made a couple hundred just that one night in Phoenix. Too bad you and Waco ran out before you could collect your share. We had a potential gold mine there. Isn't that right, Sherry?"

She nodded, and when she spoke, her voice was a tortured whisper. Clint did not even want to think of what they had done to her, so he turned back to the outlaw. "Sheriff Rankin will go down in history as the man who outgunned me. Doesn't that bother you at all?"

"Naw. Why should it?"

"Because killing me will make him rich and famous. The women will flock to him."

"Rankin better tell the newspaper that it was me who got the drop on you."

"He won't. Why should he? He'd be a fool to give you any credit."

Texas Bob thought about that real hard. "Not fair," he muttered.

"Then give me a gun and let's see who is really the best."

"You want a gun?" He laughed and pulled Waco's out of its holster that was slung over the bedpost. He pitched the gun about five feet from Clint. "Go for it."

"What kind of a chance would I have?"

The outlaw laughed. "It's the best chance you are going to get. You can either die reaching for that gun or not. Doesn't matter to me. Either way, I'm going to kill you.''

Clint took a deep, steadying breath. There was no way he could grab that weapon and fire before Texas Bob got at least three shots into him. But men had lived to kill other men with three bullet holes in them.

It was a slim chance, but Clint knew it was the only chance he had and that he was going to take it.

TWENTY-NINE

Sherry drove her fingers at Texas Bob's eyes, raking the flesh clear down to his jawline. The outlaw shouted, backhanded her, and tried to unleash a bullet at the Gunsmith all in one motion.

He failed. His first shot was wide, and before he could trigger off a second round, Clint had a gun in his hand and was making it do the kind of magic he had always used when the chips were down and his life was at stake. His motion was so quick that the gun seemed to come up in a blur, and then he fired—just once. Texas Bob Hadley was slammed back against the headboard, and he was dead even before he slumped over and pitched across the floor.

Clint was on his feet and pulling Sherry up. He held her only a moment before he said gently, "I blame myself for this. I should never have allowed you to come into town alone."

He smiled and lifted her chin. "Come on, let's get the hell out of here while we can."

She nodded, grabbed an armful of clothes, and started to dress, but Clint shook his head. "I'm afraid there is no time for that."

"But—"

Clint yanked a blanket off the bed. "Wrap yourself in that and come along. You can dress later."

"Where? On a running horse?"

She pretended to be angry, but Clint could see that she was in just as much a hurry as he was to get out of this hated room where she had been so badly abused.

She shot a look at Texas Bob Hadley that said that she was glad he was dead, and then they were moving out into the narrow, dimly lit hallway.

Clint locked the door behind him, knowing Waco and Rankin would hesitate for a few moments before knocking it down and rushing inside to face the Gunsmith. "We'll never make it down the stairs and out through the lobby," he said, looking in both directions. "We are going to have to locate a fire escape or a way to get into the alley. I am getting to know them pretty well in Tucson by now."

They hurried down the hallway and found that it ended in a bathroom with a big iron tub, soap, and buckets.

"We are trapped," Clint said, turning back into the hall. "We are going to have to go through another room."

The first door he grabbed was locked. Clint started to move on to the next, but then he heard shouts in the lobby below and knew that time had just about run out. He threw his shoulder to the door, discovering that it was sore.

"Give me a hand," he said.

Sherry dropped her bundle of clothes and threw herself at the door. The force was enough to send them crashing inside.

"Hey, what the—"

Clint saw a man sit up fast. He held a derringer in his fist, and he looked as if he knew how to use it. Clint judged the man to be a professional gambler sleeping late after a long night at the card tables.

"I'm sorry about this," Clint said, "but we are in a little trouble right at the moment and we need to borrow your window."

The man wasn't paying any attention to Clint. He was

admiring Sherry as she scooped up her clothes and then shut the door.

"Mister," he said, lowering his derringer, "if you and she are interested in a party, so am I!"

"The only party we are going to have is one where lead is being served," Clint said, rushing to the window and lifting it to peer downward. There was a big drop to the alley, and he was not sure that Sherry could make it without hurting herself.

"Grab a couple of sheets and tie them together! Quick!"

The man moved fast. Dressed in silk pajamas, he tore the covers off his bed and knotted two together, his eyes darting to Sherry as she squirmed into her dress, stockings, and shoes. She left her underclothes in a heap on the floor.

They could hear shouting down the hallway and then the sound of a door splintering, along with shouts for the Gunsmith to come out with his hands in the air.

"So you're the Gunsmith. I should have recognized you sooner, but my mind was on her," he said, handing Clint the two sheets she had knotted together.

"Sorry, but there is no time for introductions. Sherry, let's go!"

The woman took hold of the sheet and threw a pretty but bruised leg over the sill. "Long way down," she said, taking a deep breath and hesitating with uncertainty.

"We'll lower you as far as we can. Then drop and I think you will be all right."

Sherry nodded. They each gripped the sheets, and she disappeared over the side. Clint and the stranger lowered her right to the end of the sheet, and then he felt the weight release. He looked out the window to see her writhing on the ground, and no one had to tell Clint that she landed wrong and was injured.

"Your turn," the gambler said, glancing down at Sherry. "Damn shame about her. Hope you land better. Just try to get out of range. I'll see if I can delay them a moment or two."

They heard racing steps in the hallway. Clint nodded. "Thanks. I live through this, I owe you one. What is your name?"

"Dirk Winston and you don't owe me anything. You're the Gunsmith and you saved my brother's life once. Long story for another day. Good luck!"

Clint went over the side and lowered himself on the tangle of sheets until he heard a ripping sound. Then he let go and dropped. Hitting the ground, he rolled and came up on his feet, slightly shaken but otherwise fine.

"Run!" Sherry cried. "I think my ankle is broken so leave me!"

"Not a chance." Clint bent down, scooped her up, and began to run. He covered thirty feet before the bullets began to scream down the alley. But by then, he had disappeared in shadows and was heading back to O'Ginty's where Duke was waiting.

They could ride double. That horse of his was strong and fast enough to carry them to the adobe chapel. After that, they could dig in and make a stand against whatever Rankin threw their way.

THIRTY

Clint and Sherry raced out of town, and it was not until they were within a hundred yards of the adobe chapel that the first shot was fired at them. By then, they were far out of rifle range. The Legend Maker caught Sherry when she tumbled from Duke. He took one look at her brusied and swollen face, and his lips pressed tightly together in white fury.

"Who did this to you?"

"Texas Bob Hadley and Waco," she said weakly, "but Texas Bob is already dead. Clint had to kill him before we could escape."

They hurried into the chapel and were joined by Jenny. "Thank God, you are all right!"

"Sherry's ankle is broken," Clint said quickly. "We are going to have to get her to a doctor as soon as we can. But right now, I think we had better worry about the sheriff and his deputies."

As if punctuating his concern, a rifle slug ate itself meanly into the adobe, and that sent Clint and the rest of them scrambling for their weapons.

"Just hold your fire until I shoot," Clint ordered. "They are still a long way out of rifle range."

There were eight riders led by Rankin. Clint recognized all of the man's deputies plus Waco. When Clint sent a warning shot that buzzed past them, they pulled in their horses until they were bunched and milling around in a tight knot.

"What are they going to do?" Jenny asked.

Clint shook his head. "Beats me. One thing I am sure of is that they aren't stupid enough to charge across that open ground into our rifle fire. If I were them, I'd wait us out until it got dark and then come busting in."

"Gunsmith! Can you hear me? This is Sheriff John Rankin, and I want to talk!"

Clint smiled coldly. "Might as well listen to what he has to say."

Jenny grabbed his sleeve. "He is not to be trusted."

"I know that. I'll be carrying a rifle, and if he tries to kill me, I'll do my best to get him first."

Clint moved into the doorway. He paused to glance over at Sherry who was in great pain. The Legend Maker was cradling her in his lap, and Clint knew that they had to get a doctor as soon as possible to inspect that ankle and set it properly.

"Oscar," he said, checking the Winchester carbine he had chosen, "you better get up here and stand ready."

"Sure." The easterner kissed Sherry on the cheek and then came to stand beside the door.

"She is in a lot of pain, Gunsmith."

"I know. Maybe I can talk Rankin into sending a doctor out here."

"Small chance. That man doesn't know the word mercy exists."

"It's worth asking for." Clint pulled his hat down low over his eyes. "If they open fire on me, then you shoot back. But if it looks as if I am finished, then you and the women give up. They won't dare harm you, not with half the town watching."

What Clint said was true. The townspeople had come to stand on the edge of the desert and watch the impending battle. And while Rankin might be able to convince them that he had acted well within his rights as their sheriff to kill the Gunsmith, he could not possibly fool anyone into thinking that the easterner, Jenny Neal, and Sherry were equally as life-threatening.

"Damn," Oscar whispered, "I don't know how this is going to work out, but it will make a hell of a show on stage. Look at that panorama of buildings, the men on horseback. We could get a good artist and—"

"Shut up, Oscar," Clint said without anger. "Just keep quiet and be ready for whatever happens. This time it's for real."

"Maybe I should go out there now with you?"

"Bad idea. Sherry needs you and so does Jenny."

"I know. But I'm not afraid of them."

Clint smiled grimly. "You should be."

He went back and got Duke again. The animal was eager to run, and when Clint stepped up into the saddle, Jenny rushed to his side.

"If John wants me back in return for your life, say yes."

Clint reached down and touched her face. "I promise you this," he said softly, "that man will never again lay a hand on you, Jenny."

Then, before she could say another word, Clint rode out to meet the sheriff and to see what kind of a deal was on his mind. Whatever it was, Clint was sure that it would include his return to jail as well as Jenny Neal's promise of marriage.

Neither was acceptable.

Clint pulled Duke up and cradled the Winchester across his forearm. At eight-to-one odds, he did not want to get any nearer than a comfortable shouting range.

Rankin, however, had another opinion, and when he realized that Clint was coming no closer, he whispered something to Phil and Waco and then urged his horse forward.

That was fine with Clint. One against one. He had no fear of this man, nor did he trust him to act predictably. Rankin was wild, a man who acted on impulse and emotion rather than studied reason. He was like a ticking clock whose alarm might go off at any moment with violent results.

The man stopped twenty feet away. He looked thinner than Clint had remembered, and he wore a three-day growth of beard. There were dark circles under his eyes, and something told Clint that this man was stretched as tight as barbed wire, and when that stuff snapped, someone was going to get hurt.

"Jenny is in there, isn't she?"

"That's right."

"Was she the one who you brought out of town just now?"

"No. It was Sherry. She has a broken ankle that needs a doctor's attention."

"I want to see Jenny."

Clint shifted the Winchester to his left hand, while his right strayed close to his gun. "She realizes now that you had her husband set up for that bank robbery. You are the reason he is dead."

"That's a lie, Gunsmith. A bald lie." The man's denial lacked any conviction whatsoever.

"Is it? Where did you hide the money? Under your office floor? Out in the desert under some rock? You couldn't go out and spend it. Everyone in Tucson knows your salary. They'd have been immediately suspicious."

Suddenly and inexplicably, Rankin laughed out loud.

"Damn, you have it all figured out, haven't you, Gunsmith? All you need is some proof."

"That's right."

"You'll never get it from me. The fact of the matter is that I have you over a barrel. If you should outdraw me—which you won't—there goes any chance of you getting out of a prison sentence; if I outdraw you, you have nothing to worry about. You can't win!"

"That's one way of looking at it," Clint said. "But I have one other alternative you overlooked."

Rankin's smile melted. "What is that?"

Grinning, Clint said, "It's the one I am going to take right now, so you might as well fill your hand."

The expression of confusion on Rankin's face turned to one of choked fury. "I'm too fast for you to pick your shots!"

"Draw and let's find out."

Rankin went for his gun. His hand blurred downward and he was fast, but Clint had faced faster men. His own gun was up and booming. His first bullet shattered Rankin's gunhand, and his second did the same to the man's right shoulder. John Rankin bellowed in pain and was thrown from his horse as it whirled and ran.

Then, as the deputies and Waco charged forward, Clint was swinging Duke around and racing back to the adobe. Rankin would live to see courtroom justice, and he would never threaten anyone again with a gun.

Now, Clint thought as he reached the chapel and landed on the run to take cover, all we have to do is to stay alive and find a way to make the man confess.

THIRTY-ONE

They opened fire, and because Clint was the only marksman among them, it was mostly just a roar of smoke and flying bullets. Clint shot two men out of their saddles and made sure that one of them was Waco; that was enough to send the rest into a full retreat.

"We did it!" Oscar cried, jumping up and down, then hurling his derby to the earth, and stomping on it with joy. "By God, we actually did it!"

He looked happy enough to start a jig. Clint was more subdued. He said, "We can expect another attack after dark and then it might be another story entirely."

Oscar's grin died on his lips. He picked up his ruined derby and then punched the crown back into its original shape before he went over to visit Sherry who was white with pain.

"I don't want her to have to suffer long," he said. "I want to take her to see the doctor right now."

Clint thought it over. With Rankin badly wounded, the group out there would be almost leaderless. "All right," he said, glancing at Sherry. "The three of you go ahead."

"But what about you?" Jenny Neal cried. "We can't leave you alone against them!"

"I'll slip out right after dark. By the time they realize that I'm gone, I hope to have this mess wrapped up and be able to provide Judge Wilson with enough evidence to see that Rankin doesn't bother anyone for a long, long time."

"I can help you," Jenny said. "Please!"

"All right," he answered. "Oscar, meet us at Jenny's house tonight about an hour after sunset. We are going to have to act swiftly, but with any luck at all, I think this trouble will all be over soon."

Clint and Jenny watched them ride toward the remainder of Rankin's posse with more than a little apprehension. With half of Tucson watching, Clint felt the pair was in no immediate danger, but then he saw the Legend Maker gesturing angrily toward Sherry's ankle. Some of the townspeople seemed to get involved, and after a few tense moments, the confrontation was over. Oscar and Sherry were allowed to pass into Tucson without further delay.

The afternoon went by very slowly. Heat waves shimmered across the desert floor, and Clint and Jenny passed the time engaged in idle conversation about what each of them was going to do if they survived this trouble. Clint was for finding a cool mountain stream or lake and camping beside it through the remaining heat of the summer, while Jenny seemed optimistic that she could return to her millinery shop and continue to support herself.

"I thought I wanted to get married again soon," she told Clint, "but not anymore. It will be years before I trust a man other than yourself."

Clint smiled. "It will take just as long as it takes for the first good man to come by and catch your eye and your heart, Jenny. But why don't you try to pick someone besides a lawman?"

"I suppose I should." She looked up at Clint. "Do you really believe that you can prove that John Rankin was behind that bank holdup?"

"I hope so because he is guilty. And he has his share of the money stashed away somewhere. Any ideas on where to start looking for it?"

"I am afraid not. But if it helps any, I remember that the bills were all hundreds and that most of them were marked. There were also a few gold and stock certificates."

"That does help. So all we have to do is to locate them. The thing that is going to be tough to prove is that Rankin killed Sean O'Ginty—or had him killed."

"You'll find a way."

Clint said nothing. But he sure hoped Jenny was right.

Clint did not wait for the expected attack. Instead, he and Jenny climbed onto Duke and left right after dark. Within twenty minutes they were back at Jenny's house, and Oscar's gentle rapping on a windowpane came not ten minutes later.

"How's Sherry?" they both asked.

"She's going to be all right," the easterner said, mopping his brow of sweat. "The doctor said it was a crack rather than a fracture, but your bullets sure tore up Sheriff Rankin. He was in surgery almost two hours while the doctor dug a bullet out of his shoulder, and his gunhand is ruined."

"As long as he lives," Clint said without sympathy, "he got better than he deserved. Where is he now?"

Oscar peered around the pulled curtains as if expecting to be attacked any moment. "He's at O'Ginty's Saloon, upstairs in the office."

"But why there?"

"I don't know. After the surgery, they waited until just after dark to move the sheriff out the back door so that no one would see where they were taking him. It wasn't easy to follow them without being seen, but I managed.''

"Nice work," Clint said. "Now, what about the deputies? I suppose they have all gone out to attack me at the chapel. They are probably there right this very minute.''

"Guess again. Phil and the others are sticking to O'Ginty's Saloon like a flea to a mangy dog. I think we underestimated them; they know you are coming after their boss, and they want to be ready to give you a real welcome party.''

"Damn!" Clint whispered. "I was hoping to get to Rankin and be done with this without any further fighting.''

"Then you are in for a big disappointment because to get to Rankin you still have to go through at least three or four men.''

Clint frowned. "Jenny, did your husband have a collection of guns and rifles?''

"Yes," she said, leading him into a small but very comfortable parlor. "He kept them in perfect condition. They are in that rack. Take whatever you need.''

Clint chose a sawed-off, double-barreled shotgun that looked mean enough to blow down a barn all by itself. He broke it open, made sure it was loaded, and then handed it to Oscar. "You pull this off, you can be your own legend tonight.''

"What do you want me to do?" he asked, paling a little but squaring his narrow shoulders.

"Come in the back way when I come in the front. The alley door will be locked. Find something to break the lock or saw the lock off and come in exactly at midnight.''

"But—"

"I'll be depending on you, Oscar. If you can't break the damned lock, then use both barrels and blast the damned thing off. Step inside, reload, and come on through. When you reach the second door, kick it open and blow out every lamp you see hanging from the ceiling. I want that place dark when I come flyin' in the front door."

"Then what do I do?"

Clint smiled. "You will notice right away that everyone hits the floor whenever a man with a sawed-off shotgun opens fire. By the time they recover from the surprise, I expect you will have sent the place into darkness. If you haven't, I'll finish the job and be up those stairs as fast as I can."

Oscar took a deep breath. "Now, that," he said, "would really make one hell of a stage performance!"

"If you pull your part off so that I can reach the upstairs office, then I'll go on stage with you once before I quit Tucson for good."

"Will you put that in writing?"

"No," Clint said, "but I'll give you my hand on it, and that is worth a whole lot more than any contract to me."

They shook then: two men totally different and suddenly and totally dependent upon each other. Clint knew that the Legend Maker would somehow manage to accomplish his task—but he could not have nor would he have even tried a month ago. The man had markedly changed for the better. Oh, sure, he was still a big talker, a showman, and a braggart, but now, maybe for the first time in his life, he would really have something to brag about, something to allow him to look any legendary gunfighter or outlaw in the eye and know how it actually feels to hold a gun or a rifle in his fist and have his life and maybe the life of a friend hanging in the balance.

Oscar was a changed man, a hundred times better, and Clint hoped with all his heart that he lived to marry Sherry.

Clint kissed Jenny good-bye, and then he and Oscar headed for O'Ginty's Saloon. That was the place this thing had all started. Maybe it was right that it also be the place where everything ended—one way or the other.

"Good luck, Oscar."

The man swallowed dryly. "Thanks, I'll need it."

"You'll do fine," Clint assured him. "Just try to put two blasts at the lights. That is a real gun in your fists. You don't even need to aim the damn thing except over everyone's head. It is guaranteed to do the rest for you."

Oscar nodded and started to move away.

"Legend Maker?"

Oscar turned in the semidarkness, his face looking worried but determined. "Yeah?"

"Tomorrow night, you and I are going to stage a live performance right at O'Ginty's Saloon, and the place will be packed. And you know what?"

The man shook his head, a broad smile forming on his lips.

"You," Clint said, "are going to be not only the announcer, but my co-star."

Oscar seemed to rise up a little taller and stand a little straighter. "Yeah," he said, his voice thick with emotion. "No more bozo for me, huh?"

"That's right," Clint said softly as he disappeared into the darkness.

THIRTY-TWO

Clint hauled out his watch and flared a match against the heel of his boot. It was just a couple of minutes shy of midnight, and Oscar ought to be ready to break through the back door of O'Ginty's Saloon. Clint was nervous, but not because he had any doubts about his own ability to fight his way through the saloon and up those steps to Dennis's office. No, his nervousness was because he was worried that Oscar might get himself killed.

But there was no other way that Clint could think of to reach the upstairs office without a full-scale shoot-out, one that might kill a lot of innocent people.

He dropped the match in the street and moved purposefully toward the front of the saloon. Clint could hear the piano player, hear, too, the raucous laughter from within. He could not help but wonder why the deputies had seen fit to bring Sheriff Rankin to a saloon for safekeeping. It seemed a damned unlikely choice for a recovery room.

Clint paused for a moment beside the front window of the saloon and peered inside, hoping to see Phil and the other deputies and learn exactly where they were positioned. The saloon, however, was filled with men, and the light was too poor to identify any of the deputies. He could count on a couple of them being upstairs with the wounded sheriff. Probably another one or two would be close to the foot of the stairs, and that would about account for the lot of them.

Pretending to be drunk, Clint pulled his hat down low

over his face and sort of bounced along the wall toward the front doors. There he paused and leaned against the wall as if trying to keep his balance. To anyone who passed, he looked just like another drunken cowboy who had spent all his money but still was trying to figure out a way to have one more shot of whiskey for the road.

Several men passed to go inside, and each time the doors swung open, Clint moved across them to peer inside. He thought he saw two deputies by the stairs, and one was stationed not less than five feet away from him cradling a shotgun of his own.

Suddenly, Clint heard a wild rebel yell, and then, bigger than life, the Legend Maker jumped through the rear door, and raising the shotgun to his shoulder, he opened fire. The gun sounded like a military cannon inside that saloon. It raked the ceiling of the room from back to front and plunged the establishment into almost total darkness. Men shouted amid the crashing of tables, chairs, and glasses as everyone hit the floor.

Clint stepped inside just as the deputy beside him raised his own shotgun to fire across the room at Oscar. It was a heartless decision for the man to reach, for almost certainly there would be innocent customers killed by the blast; Clint momentarily forgot about the stairs. He threw his body at the deputy, and the shotgun spat fire and gunpowder into the floor. Clint twisted the shotgun out of the man's fist and sent its barrel crashing down across the deputy's skull.

Flashes split the dark interior of the saloon and men shouted in fear and anger. Clint got to his feet and charged down the long mahogany bar toward the stairs. Coming from the outside darkness, he had a few seconds of advantage due to his night vision. He intended to make the most of it.

The two deputies by the stairs were groping for a

target and Clint used the shotgun's barrel twice more to send them crashing to the floor, stunned and harmless. He struck the stairs running, and when he reached the top landing, he grabbed the door and threw it open.

Sheriff John Rankin was propped up in his bed, face white and eyes tortured with pain.

He had a gun in his good fist and it bucked twice, but he was firing with his left hand and not his right. In his weakened state, he was trembling. Both shots went wild and Clint leveled his gun on the man and shouted, "Drop it!"

Rankin cursed viciously and tried to steady his gun. That is when Clint returned fire. His bullet smashed into the gun and punched it back hard against Rankin's chest. The man cried out in pain, and Clint grabbed him by the shirt and hauled him erect.

"You had Sheriff Neal set up to be killed and you staged that holdup! Admit it!"

"No!" Rankin hissed.

Clint half dragged, half carried the wounded sheriff out of the room to the stairs. The bartender down below had gotten some candles lit, and now Clint stared down at a room filled with angry and confused men among overturned tables and chairs. The only man who seemed unaffected by the noise, death, and confusion was Oscar who calmly went about the task of reloading his shotgun before moving toward the stairs with a grin on his face.

"Listen!" Clint yelled down to the bar patrons below. "I meant no innocent man among you harm, but Sheriff Rankin here is a murderer who had his boss killed and then also killed Sean O'Ginty!"

Rankin tried to struggle. His head rolled back and forth, and as all eyes strained toward him, they saw

Clint cock back the hammer of his gun and place it against the man's forehead.

"Tell them the truth or I will kill you right here and now," he said. "Confess or you have one more second of life!"

"I swear I didn't order Sean O'Ginty killed. Wasn't . . . wasn't necessary. But . . . yeah, yeah I did set up the bank robbery," Rankin said. "I wanted Sheriff Neal's job and his woman."

"And the money, where is the money?"

"Phil and—"

He never finished. Phil leaped out from the shadows, and his gun bucked fire and death. Clint felt Rankin's body take the first bullet and then a second that had his own name on it. He released the dying sheriff and tried to twist and fire, but before he could, the Legend Maker's shotgun was booming once more. Two blasts at almost point-blank range caught Phil in the chest and sent him catapulting backward over an upended poker table as everyone in the saloon hit the floor a second time.

Clint lowered the sheriff to the landing. The man was almost dead; it was amazing that his heart still continued to beat feebly. Clint stared into his glazing eyes. "Phil and who?" he whispered. "Who else is behind all of this?"

For an instant, the dying man's eyes seemed to focus and shine; his lips formed a single word. Then as Clint lowered his ear to the man's face, Rankin whispered once more, louder and with his last dying rush of breath.

Clint eased the man down on the carpet. "Thanks," he said. "Thanks for that much at least."

He stood up then and reloaded his gun. "You're all

going to be witnesses to Judge Wilson. Oscar, please go find the judge and the mayor and ask them to come and learn that before he died Sheriff Rankin admitted that he was the cause of the bank holdup and the death of Sheriff Neal."

"But not Sean O'Ginty." Oscar shook his head. "Then who—"

"His brother," Clint said. "Dennis hated and killed Sean because he was bigger, stronger, handsomer, far more popular, and successful."

Clint shook his head. "Hell, Oscar, unless I miss my guess, Dennis O'Ginty was behind everything and Sheriff Rankin was little more than a tool he used to achieve ownership of this saloon as well as revenge for years of insults and shabby treatment."

Oscar nodded. "You can almost pity little Dennis O'Ginty whom Sean treated like dirt."

"Maybe he knew all along that Dennis was capable of murder. Maybe—maybe he was trying to intimidate Dennis to the point where he was no longer man enough to seek revenge for all the humiliation and insults."

Clint shook his head and started down the stairs. He laid his hand on Oscar's shoulder. "You handled yourself like a true gunfighter, a man of action. Never look up to anyone for his bravery again. You've won your spurs and your own small place in history."

Oscar was clearly too moved to speak. Then, still holding the shotgun, he reloaded it once more and went to find the mayor and Judge Wilson.

Clint pulled twenty dollars out of his pocket and slammed it on the bar. "For the inconvenience," he said, "I want to buy every man here a round of drinks on the house. Your best!"

"Yes, sir, Gunsmith!"

Clint drank his own whiskey neat as men crowded

around just to be able to say that they drank with him. He waited until Oscar returned with the mayor, the judge, and even the city editor who frantically took notes while man after man testified to the admission that Sheriff Rankin had made just before he died of his wounds.

Judge Wilson came to Clint and bought a round of drinks, which surprised everyone because the man was known for his stinginess. "Mr. Adams," he said, leaning back from the bar, "I salute you for your bravery and for the service you have done for Tucson as well as for upholding the tradition of the law in the finest sense of the word."

"Thank you," Clint said quietly. He could not quite forgive the judge for sentencing him to two years in prison for such a minor case of mistaken identity, and yet he was content in the belief that Judge Wilson would be more evenhanded with his sentences in the future and not ever be swayed by a sheriff again. "I believe in justice for everyone, and I know you do, too."

The judge cleared his throat. "Absolutely, my friend! And now that you have cleared your name of all charges, and we know that Dennis O'Ginty is the evil purveyor of so much wrongdoing, you must seek him out and apprehend the scoundrel!"

"I suppose he'll hang for the death of his brother?"

"Of course! And for his part in the death of our dearly departed Sheriff Neal and the bank manager! Justice must be swift and unwavering when it comes to murder."

"Yeah," Clint said, finishing his drink.

The editor caught his arm. "I just have to get a full story from you for our paper, Mr. Adams. Please, it'll just take—"

"I'm sorry," Clint said. "Right now, there is still

some unfinished business to attend. I'll see you in the morning."

"But—"

"You have my word on that, sir. Now, if you will excuse me?"

The editor nodded and stepped back. "Of course. Excuse me for being so insistent. It is just that it is not often that a small town editor like myself has the chance to write a piece of history."

Clint had nothing more to say as he moved outside and then stood for a moment taking in the warm desert air. He took a deep breath and then he headed for his horse.

Dennis O'Ginty would be on the run. And since there were no stages out tonight and he must have been present to hear all the gunfire, it did not take great intelligence to reason that the man had to have departed town within the last few minutes.

Clint mounted Duke, knowing that he would find Dennis O'Ginty, and then he would offer him a choice—go to trial or die.

The choice was regrettable but very, very simple.

THIRTY-THREE

The night was a pale gray curtain overlaid with a field of glittering stars. The moon was framed in a silvery aureole that lay as soft as candlelight across the oven-hot desert floor. Clint had chosen to ride north toward Phoenix, for that was the real gateway to opportunity and the one most likely to be taken by the young murderer.

He let Duke gallop easily in a long, sweeping glide, which was rocking-chair easy and yet which could devour the miles. Within an hour, Clint could see the pale mist of dust rising up toward the moon from the road.

It was Dennis O'Ginty, and the man was driving a buckboard, driving it hard with the single-mindedness of a man bent on survival and escape. Clint narrowed the distance steadily until he was within a hundred yards of the bouncing buckboard, and then he unholstered his gun and fired a warning shot into the sky.

Dennis had been unaware of being followed; he had probably thought that he would have at least a day or two head start. When he heard Clint's gun, he twisted around in the seat, and then he began whipping the two-horse team, which he had already been pushing too long and too hard.

The horses were coated with lather and breathing hard, and though they did manage a brief burst of speed, they were incapable of more. Clint was determined to spare the animals any further suffering. He let Duke have his head, and within moments he was alongside the wagon and shouting for the Irishman to pull over or be shot.

Dennis hauled the team in slowly, but before the buckboard was fully stopped, he jumped off the far side of the wagon, hit the dirt, rolled, then climbed to his feet, and began to race into the desert.

Clint let him go because, on foot, there was no escape. He dismounted and climbed into the buckboard to open a small trunk. There was plenty of moonlight to see that it contained several thousand dollars, all in hundred-dollar bills, along with a thick stack of gold and stock certificates.

"That's it then," he said, watching the silhouette of Dennis O'Ginty jerk its pathetic way across the desert floor.

He sat on the buckboard letting his legs dangle over the sides. He heard a coyote howl at the moon, and he thought about how he did not want to return to the desert again for a long, long time.

Clint also thought about Dennis and how he had been so shamefully insulted, ridiculed, and humiliated before other men by his very own brother. Perhaps any man would turn mean and murderous under those circumstances. But then he thought about how this was a free country, one where no man was the slave of another. That meant that if he were treated unjustly, he could walk out and find a better opportunity elsewhere. Clint guessed no one would ever know exactly why Sean had treated his younger brother like dirt, but the thing that was important was that Dennis had chosen to kill, rather than seek a better life by standing on his own two feet.

And besides all that, there was the matter of Sheriff Neal and the bank manager who were dead before their time, and Dennis O'Ginty had the bank's money to prove he had been responsible for that, too. And last, as if Clint needed more convincing, he remembered the way Dennis had leered when he had spoken about Sherry and how she had been auditioned for a job, which meant he raped and abused her to satisfy his carnal desires.

Clint hopped off the buckboard and climbed back on Duke. He trotted out into the desert after a man who had suffered but who had also caused much suffering and death.

By the time he overtook Dennis, the man was staggering with fatigue and wild with hysteria. Clint circled around to come to a stop before him. "You can't run away any longer, Dennis. I have to take you back."

"No!" the man screamed as he swayed to a halt. "I'll hang for sure!"

"No doubt, but that is up to the judge."

Dennis yanked a small handgun out of his pocket, and Clint drew his own weapon. "Don't do it," he warned the man on the ground. "I don't want to have to kill you."

"You don't, Gunsmith. I'm not going to die one day at a time waiting to be hung. So ride away," he said, turning the weapon to his own heart.

Clint studied the man for a long moment. He wanted to ask him why he had not gone away before hatred twisted his mind to the point of murder. But before he could ask, Dennis O'Ginty pulled the trigger.

THIRTY-FOUR

True to his word, Clint allowed himself to be cast in one more stage appearance with the Legend Maker. He even consented to play the murdering deputy named Phil, while letting Oscar play the Gunsmith. It was strange portraying a villain and letting someone else fill his shoes. It was all done with high spirits and in great humor, and the Tucson audience that packed O'Ginty's Saloon loved every minute of the action-packed performance.

Oscar paid Clint another hundred dollars, which was good because he was almost broke. The eastern promoter also gave Clint a handful of cigars and pulled him aside to say, "Tell me the truth now, Gunsmith. Tonight, up on that little stage, didn't you feel the thrill of the applause, the blood-pounding excitement of a live audience when it howls its appreciation for your talent? Admit it, my friend! Come join Sherry and me, and we will excite the entire eastern seaboard!"

Clint laughed outright but did admit that it was sort of fun to see himself making so many people laugh.

"Of course, it was! I could design an entire—"

Clint poked one of the Legend Maker's own cigars into his mouth. He stuck out his hand. "I've done my part. Now, how about that contract I signed when I was in jail?"

"What about it?" Oscar asked innocently.

"I'd like it back. I'd feel better tearing it up."

"Sorry, it's in a bank vault in Phoenix."

186

Clint heaved a deep sigh. "No matter. This was the finish of my stage career. We part good friends, though. I wish you luck."

At that moment, Sherry came up to them. Slipping her arm around Oscar's plump waist, she said, "I heard that and I wanted to explain that Oscar and I plan on making our own luck. Now that we are a little famous, we figure we can do plenty well on our own."

"You mean no more of The Great Wild West Outlaws and Gunfighters Show?"

"That's right," Sherry said emphatically. "I think Oscar and I both deserve to have the chance to become legitimate thespians in our own right. We can both quote Shakespeare and with a little practice, I believe we can play the western theaters for as long as we choose and give them high comedy as well as great drama. What do you think, Gunsmith?"

Clint wholeheartedly agreed. "I think you owe yourselves that chance and that you'll succeed if that is what you really want to do."

Oscar nodded. "It is. No more bozo for me. A solid actor is what I want to become."

"Then I wish you great success and happiness." Clint moved outside to where Jenny Neal was waiting. There was also a huge crowd of well-wishers who included the judge, the mayor, the editor, and about every other citizen of importance in Tucson, all of them deeply grateful for his ridding the city of a corrupt sheriff and his deputies.

"Good-bye Jenny," he said, tilting her chin up to his face. "I hope you sell a million hats before you're done and that the right man comes along."

"He already has—twice."

"Uh-uh. Once. I never was the right man. But

another one will soon catch your fancy. As beautiful as you are, there will be a steady parade of eligible bachelors strutting past your door. Just pick one in a safe line of work and then have a couple of fine, sturdy children."

"Can I name our first son after you?"

"I'd be deeply honored," he said, meaning it. Clint kissed her then, full and deeply and right in front of the townspeople. Grown men smiled, young girls tittered, and the boys smirked with childhood devilment.

Clint did not care. Maybe, he thought as he swung onto Duke's back, a lot of women would want to buy a new hat from a lady who had been rescued, romanced, and then publicly kissed by the Gunsmith.

The idea brought a laugh bubbling up from his throat as he waved farewell and galloped toward the high, cool mountains.